TEQUILA,
LEMON, AND SALT

D0973662

TEQUILA, LEMON, AND SALT

From Baja... tales of love, faith – and magic

DANIEL REVELES

SUNBELT PUBLICATIONS
San Diego, California

Cover and book design by Laurel Miller
Project management by Jennifer Redmond
Printed in the United States of America

Sunbelt Publications, Inc.
P.O. Box 191126
San Diego, CA 92159-1126
(619) 258-4911
(619) 258-4916 FAX
www.sunbeltbooks.com

10 09 08 07   5 4 3 2

LIBRARY OF CONGRESS CATALOGING-IN-PUBLICATION DATA

Reveles, Daniel
Tequila, lemon, and salt : from Baja tales of love and faith / Daniel Reveles.-- 1st ed.
    p. cm.
ISBN 0-932653-65-0
    1. Tecate (Mexico)--Fiction. 2. Baja California (Mexico)--Fiction. 3. Mexican-American Border Region--Fiction. I. Title.

PS3568.E785T47 2005
813'.54--dc22
                    2004019380

Cover Painting "Bar Diana" by Gabriel Adame

Every man should have a son, plant a tree, and write a book.
— Persian proverb

This is for Mark, my son, my tree, my book.

Acknowledgments

I am forever indebted to Valerie Ross, my Maxwell Perkins, who by now has read over a million manuscript pages and put in a million arduous hours of editorial genius in the course of producing this, the third collection of *novelas* from Tecate. I never would have attempted it without you! Special thanks to Michael Ross who on more than one occasion dropped what he was doing to come to Mexico and save me from an emotionally disturbed computer. *Un abrazo para* Cheryl Woodruff who started the whole enchilada. This is also my opportunity to thank Joe Medina and Homer Lusk, two dedicated professors at Grossmont College who effectively lure non-readers out of the dark and into the bright world of reading, using my books for bait. *Gracias* to Ronnie Rosa, friend, neighbor, and genial host at Rancho Tecate Resort who rescued the villa (and several manuscripts) with his water tanker when the flames got high during the big fire. There will always be a warm place in my heart for Doña Fortuna who in her mysterious way led me by the hand and delivered me to Sunbelt, and my new friends: Lowell and Diana Lindsay, and Jennifer Redmond, *amiga encantadóra y editora quintaesencial.*

Contents

Aperitivo

I just knew you'd like it here at La Fonda. They do a great steak ranchero. Recognize the song the mariachis are playing? It's *Una Copa Mas* by Chucho Navarro. Can you hear the violins weeping for a love that might have been? Does the silvery trumpet stir memories carefully wrapped and stored away in a corner of your heart? Listen! *Pour me another for a love that couldn't be/pour me another to ease my breaking heart. Ay ay ay!* Dip your tortilla chip in the salsa at your own peril. Ahh — the margaritas are here — *salud*!

I have so many stories to tell you, so many people I want you to meet, I don't really know where to begin. You'll have a chance to see your neighbors as they really are, a chance to look into their homes and into their hearts. The characters you're going to meet today are not cartoons. They are the real Mexicans that I see and talk to every day. You don't need to speak Spanish. Your smile will do just as well. And you mustn't expect to find that quality of state you call reality. We discovered long ago that reality is the major cause of stress and we've succeeded in eradicating it. And put your watch away. The ever-rolling river of Time went dry years ago. Here in Tecate time no longer exists.

Was I always this loose? *Dios mio*, no! In my first life in Los Angeles I was in bondage. Every day was a timed event. Each day was carefully scheduled. On Tuesday we scheduled Wednesday before it was born. With two radio shows to do, foreign documentaries for TV, and post-production work, every minute of every day of my life belonged to someone else. Not until I dropped everything at the zenith of my career and came to Tecate did I claim my second life. Now, when the lazy sun yawns, and peeks sleepily over the hills of Tanama, and the big red rooster tiptoes on the fence to announce a new morning, the day belongs to me.

It took some adjustment, of course. The word schedule is unknown here. It doesn't even appear in the dictionary as a single word. No one bothers to make an appointment because nobody is going to bother to keep it anyway. I spent two years trying to find Raul, head of the electric company, to see about getting connected. I made several "appointments" with the phantom who was never in his office at the appointed hour or even on the appointed day. By sheer Providence I ran across this human drinking fountain one afternoon walking across the plaza. I quickly invited him into the Diana for an afternoon quencher. The following week the villa was ablaze with lights. I am presently going through a similar process with the telephone company.

But I no longer froth at the mouth when the driver of the car in front of me stops in the middle of the street and lowers his window to have a pleasant chat with a friend who happens to be coming in the opposite direction. And I've learned to go around the potholes even if it means going on the wrong side of the street. It seems to work out okay, and no one seems to mind. We don't have road rage here in my pueblo.

Language was never a problem, of course. Both my parents fled the bloody Mexican Revolution and ended up in L.A. (In case you are a Border Patrol agent reading this, it was legal in those days). There, they eventually met, married, and Thursday's child came to Life's banquet. Spanish was the only language I knew or needed—until my first day of school. Learning English became a major trauma. There are some letter combinations in the English language that can do major damage to the Hispanic lingual organ. The most difficult of these to articulate is the t-sound when followed by s. Words like acts will come out sounding like acss. Other examples are that's, doughnuts, and coconuts that come out as thass, donass, and coconuss... I didn't see this as a major problem in my life until I took a girlfriend to a local fair, and handing her a bright red and white striped bag, asked, "You like peanuss?" It was a cosmic moment of enlightenment. The next day I began to work on my deficiency in elocution. It took years of careful listening and imitation of teachers and radio announcers to get it right.

I'm compelled to confess you may find us technologically challenged, as you say on the Other Side. We're so far behind you that we have no hopes of ever catching up to the most advanced nation in the world. An example: We don't have anything as advanced as those little stickers you put on your fruit at your supermarkets. Our poor checkers still have to examine the fruit, scratch their pretty heads to stimulate the neurotransmitters to advise the brain whether she is ringing up a Granny Smith or an Elberta peach. That's life in the Third World, I guess, but we seem to get by. We'll never achieve your state of development even though we live right next door. Take our space program as a case in point. Back when Mir was doing circles around our planet the Mexican space agency decided they would send a man up to rendezvous with the Russians. But the launch had to be scrubbed at the last minute when they ran into some technical difficulties getting the astronaut in the piñata. We can never catch up to you sociologically either. When a man in Tecate says, "Hey, I'm getting married next Saturday," in all probability he means a woman. We're still in the larval stage. (We didn't think women were competent enough to put an X on a ballot until 1953).

Nothing worthy of note happens in Tecate. That may be why we don't have a daily newspaper. I do remember what could have been a major news story, though. A couple of years ago Chanito's goats got loose in the plaza and did some pretty extensive trimming and pruning in the rose gardens in the plaza. That was kind of exciting. Big Nalgas Machado arrested the old man, fined him three hundred pesos and one goat. Machado barbecued the goat on his rancho and it was pretty good.

As you can see, we just don't have a lot of high drama. We don't have snipers. No one sends the Presidente Municipal a Hallmark card with a smart-ass punch line and anthrax spores. And we don't have eighth graders gunning down their teachers over some argument about an A or a B in algebra. We don't even have terrorists. The most lethal biological weapon we have is the public restrooms. That's how underdeveloped we are here. We have five churches of various denominations and none has ever been blown up. Last year we had our first bank holdup, though. Now, that was exciting. I remember the bank robbers had to push-start the getaway car. It almost didn't matter because the police car was in the garage getting new brakes. Here in Tecate you won't find a noticeable difference between reality and fantasy. I think that's why I'm here.

I want to show you everything while I've got you here. Come with me to the Saturday open air market. We can shop for groceries, bras and panties at Josefina's Secret, motor oil for your car, and beef so fresh the head is still attached. Here in Tecate we are never far from the spirit world, so if you find yourself presently in the need of the services of a reliable psychic, seer, or genuine witch, you're in the right place. If you have a problem that you think can benefit from ornithomancy, consult the Yellow-Breasted Sapsucker who does readings for ten pesos. There's Doña Lala and La Regina for spells and curses. And if you're interested in looking into future events, there's no one better than Doña Marcelina who practices scatomancy. We think of her as our local poop psychic. She employs a duck for her purpose. And I give her high marks.

Not long ago I went to her for a reading. She laid out a white plastic sheet and told me to draw a circle on it with a felt marker. She reached into a cardboard box and brought out a big fat duck with big yellow feet. She placed it in the center of the circle and began to throw out little pieces of tortilla. The duck greedily scooped them up with contented onomatopoeic parlance. *Quack, quack, quack.* In time, of course, the fowl made its contribution in the form of aromatic squiggles and splotches.

Pleased with the results, Doña Marcelina replaced the duck in the box and began the reading. She explained to me that the outer edges of the circle represented the distant future, the center of the circle, the more immediate future. She referred to the greenish splatters as "patterns of Destiny." She told me I was enjoying good health and no illness was in the immediate future. "Ah! you see this little pattern in the shape of a wing? It indicates a journey. And see this heart-shaped pattern? A stranger, a woman, probably from the Other Side, will come into your life. We shall call her Señorita X." Your standard one-size-fits-all reading, I thought, health, a journey, and a mysterious woman. "And you see this," she went on. But then her face darkened. *Oh, oh, oh.* "What is it?" I asked. "What do you see? Tell me!" She studied the disgusting patterns of Destiny for several minutes before she answered. "This broken line means you're going to lose something. Something important. But it's worse than that. Notice the line is broken in two places. That means you're going to lose it twice!"

Well, I thought, that was a new experience. I gave her fifty pesos and never thought about it again. I've always enjoyed perfect health. I did have to fly to Dallas to do a book signing so that counts as a journey. A pretty standard reading, I thought, that she and her duck could apply to anyone with fifty pesos. I always take work with me when I travel. I took the manuscript for *Tequila, Lemon, and Salt.* I never thought about Marcelina again. Until I changed planes in Phoenix and realized I had left the manuscript on the other plane! Immediately the image of Marcelina and her duck came to me. But I kept panic to a minimum. There was nothing I could do and took comfort in the fact there was a hard copy in my desk at home. The first thing I did when I got back was to look for the hard copy. It was gone. Disappeared. And now the only thing I could think of was Marcelina and her silly duck. And if Señorita X shows up, I'm a believer!

I'm sorry we won't see the human flamethrower, well known to readers of my earlier books. He took his act, shooting live flame out of his mouth like a blowtorch, down to Ensenada where the big cruise ships come in and he gets a bigger crowd. We won't see the bug man either, I'm afraid. Remember him? He's the character who used to walk around the plaza with a Mason jar filled with worms, mealybugs, cockroaches, caterpillars, and little spiders. For a coin he would pop one in his mouth and eat it rapturously. He never failed to gross out his audience. I heard he hasn't been feeling too great lately and he's staying with his mother. And I don't think he's got workman's comp.

But you will meet El Chaparro, the vaquero who comes jogging into town about this time riding a big black and white Holstein cow. Comandante Big Caca is back—meaner than ever! And Big Nalgas Machado, Tecate's fattest cop. You'll attend a couple of extraordinary weddings and watch true love prevail when the tortilla chips are down. And you'll sit in with Los Cafeteros, Tecate's Upper Chamber of Deputies who convene for coffee every morning at La Fonda to draft legislation and memoranda to Vicente Fox, El Boosh, and that *cabron* Bin Laden. Just as quickly they'll abandon world affairs and argue vehemently over the ideal sequence in which to perform the ritual of tequila, lemon, and salt. They also tell some outrageous stories.

But enough of this! Let's order another margarita and I'll tell you everything. I'll point out the locals and tell you their stories. Some are sure to induce laughter, some might put a strain on your concept of Truth, still others may provoke tears. But they're real—every one! Let me begin with a love story, the story of Salvador, a man who feared the past, and Esperanza, a beautiful young woman who feared the future.

— *Your Servidor*
Tecate, B.C.N., Mexico

Dear God

The little tinker-toy border town of Tecate, immune to the symptoms of Time, emerges from dormancy to renewed life soon after the Easter Bunny (imported from the U.S.A.) has made his appearance. Warm May breezes, scented with summer's promise, banish the gods of ice and rain and winds of winter back into the Underworld to make room for her summer guests of bee and songbird, worm and flower. The open air market nearly explodes with color under blue and red and orange canvas tarps where vendors cry their wares in song and rhyme, some with the aid of bell and chime.

Ding-a-ling-ling! "Brushes, feather dusters, and mops — a broom for every room!"

Clang, clang, clang! *"Tamales...ricos tamales de puerco!"*

In the shade of the produce tent, double-wide señoras wrapped in black shawls wend their way under garlands of garlic, red chile peppers, and bananas, squeezing and sniffing the avocados and tomatoes before dropping them into their baskets. Next to the meat market, where thirsty flies buzz around a beef carcass hanging from a wire, intimate apparel is laid out like an old-fashioned ladies' garden with banks of pink, blue, red, and yellow bras stuffed with tissue paper and arranged in long rows like puffy chrysanthemums. Panties, in pastels, solids, and prints, are set out by color in neat beds like flowering annuals. A hand-lettered piece of cardboard reads: "JOSEFINA'S SECRET."

Now, if you don't mind the crowds, come walk with me through the marketplace. There's someone I want you to meet. Her name is Esperanza and I want to tell you her story. It all started right here at the *mercado* not that long ago. I remember now it was early in June.

It was only mid-afternoon and the crowds in the narrow market lane began to thicken. Old women with bulging shopping bags, families with young children, made the pilgrimage to browse, and to gratify the whims of the palate while they shopped. Young gallants were here to buy a bouquet of roses for the girl on their arm or summon a musician to sing a love song in hopes the investment would culminate in a kiss. Street musicians were ready for them. Violins and guitars could be heard tuning up with the string basses, the silver notes of a mariachi trumpet ruffled the air, and over near twin towers of Lovly toilet paper, Alejandro doodled gay little figures on his accordion.

"Corn...sweet corn...come get your corn on the cob!" Don Ramón sang the song of the siren aided by the seductive smell of fresh corn roasting over manzanita stovewood.

Doña Balbina added her voice to the madrigal, putting everyone at market under the spicy spell of cinnamon and sugar. *"Churros...churros...ricos y calientes!"*

Shiny fish, very dead and very smelly, stared goggle-eyed at the scene from their nest of crushed ice under the fishmonger's blue tarp. Two dark men, bent over enormous cauldrons that boiled and bubbled like something out of Macbeth, were rendering pig rind into *chicharrónes*, stirring their evil brew with long wooden ladles.

Near the end of the lane, between the Watermelon Lady and Doña Marcelina (the poop psychic), Esperanza Contreras, the flower girl, carefully arranged her bouquets of fresh roses in little tin buckets by color in preparation for a busy evening. The darkest velvety reds first, then scarlet, then pink. On her other table, the deepest orange followed by golden yellow, down to cream and white. Esperanza was a bright and cheerful young woman whom God in His mysterious wisdom chose to endow with the gift of beauty. Her delicate face could easily have been done by Monet, with those big expressive eyes of polished jade and his signature ripe-strawberry mouth. Some of the old-timers in the plaza would tell you Esperanza was the most beautiful girl in Tecate—and they could not be indicted for exaggerating! Her silky hair tumbled down her back like a black waterfall. Typically, Monet had brushed a soft blush on her skin, smooth as ivory. And she had a smile that could arrest a healthy man's heart at twenty meters.

But Esperanza wasn't smiling today. It was the saddest day of her life. And today was her birthday. She felt an ache in her breast and it would have been so easy to let the tears come. Twenty-six years old today, she told herself, and I have never felt a man's lips on mine, I've never felt the warmth of a man's embrace or strolled around the plaza arm in arm with my *novio* like all the other girls. Fate has handed me a life sentence of solitary confinement, she thought. And there is no armor against Fate. Why, dear God, why? I just want what every normal woman wants. Is that so wrong?

"*Buenas tardes*, Esperanza!"

Esperanza quickly dropped her winter-gray mood and looked down at a little brown boy with a sunflower smile. He held out a brown paper bag stained with big splashy sunbursts of cooking oil. It was filled with hot *churros* glistening with sugar and cinnamon. "*Gracias*, Pepito." From her Garcia y Vega cigar box she took out a shiny coppery coin, big as a gringo silver dollar and thick as an Oreo cookie. She pressed the ten pesos into his sticky hand. Pepito didn't expect to be paid. His mother always sent a bag of hot *churros* to Esperanza. "And tell your mamá I said *Gracias!*" The first bite was just enough sugar and spice to cause her to close her eyes in delicious ecstacy. Her uncustomary attack of self-pity melted away.

"*Hola!*"

When Esperanza opened her eyes she looked down at Ofelia, a little girl of ten or so in her big sister's dress of vibrant yellow stripes with six inches of white eyelet hem. She was clutching a Styrofoam cup of hot coffee securely in both hands.

"*Gracias, mi amor.*" Esperanza made another withdrawal at the Garcia y Vega ATM and put another fat coin in the little girl's hand. "And tell your mamá I'll see her later." With wistful eyes she watched Ofelia pirouette down the lane, arms outstretched like wings, her second-hand yellow dress with the eyelet hem flaring out elegantly like a prima ballerina. It was moments like this when Esperanza felt like someone had just thrown a warm comforter over her heart. She knew every vendor, every pushcart hawker in the plaza by name. They always sent something to her from their stalls, never expecting payment. She looked up at that moment and saw old Don Tibursio, the balloon man, trolling for susceptible children in the vicinity of the candy stall. He drifted slowly under a giant cloud of bright red and yellow and green and pink and blue balloons. *Santos!* The man must be as old as Moctezuma. She could remember Don Tibursio putting a big red balloon in her little hand when her Nana brought her to play in the plaza. He would never accept the big coin her Nana tried to push into his leathery hand.

Esperanza was halfway through the *churros* and coffee when she realized the wholesale florist down the street where she bought her flowers every day hadn't delivered all the red roses she'd ordered and seeing it was Sunday, she'd better have extra. She put down her coffee and dusted sparkling sugar from her dress. Her wardrobe was consistently modest but no fashion, no style, no costume, not even a bed sheet, could ever rise to the challenge of camouflaging the exquisite young body that lived and breathed underneath. Today's simple cotton shift was the color of strawberry sherbet with cap sleeves and a cheeky little white bow at the neckline. A thin gold cross rested on her chest. She preferred dresses to pants. They made her feel more feminine. She didn't want to look like a boy. And besides, dresses were cooler. She always wore a pair of sensible flats. The white wool shawl with a built-in scarf her Nana made for her hung over the back of a chair, insurance against an evening chill. She wasn't busy yet. This was the moment to see the florist about the extra roses. Esperanza stepped off the curb and began to twist and lurch like a wooden puppet with a broken leg-string as she hobbled across the street on her deformed foot.

The horrid gait didn't embarass Esperanza. She'd walked with that grotesque limp since she first learned to walk when she was nearly two. But it never ceased to annoy her. Congenital deformity of the left foot, the doctor told her grandmother, who had raised her from the day she was born. Esperanza had no memory of her mother who died of some vague kidney disease before she was two. And she had no recollection of her father either. When her mother died her father emigrated to the Other Side and found work. To this day he faithfully sends her grandmother a postal money order the first day of every month. But Esperanza never knew their faces, never heard their voices, never felt the loving kisses and caresses showered on a baby by a mother and a father. Her Nana was her whole world. She still lived with her in the same little purple house with the pink trim and the sagging porch where she was born.

Her physical defect so early in life deprived Esperanza of the friendship of other children. When she entered kindergarten she couldn't run and skip and hop and play games with the other children and they soon played without her. While they played *roña*, chasing and screaming and tagging each other, she sat on the ground and quietly drew pictures in the dirt with a stick. She lived inside her own loneliness. And it never changed for the remainder of her life. In high school it was the same thing. She couldn't participate in sports, never went to the fiestas and the dances. Never dated. Over time, "poor Esperanza" simply had no place in the busy lives of her friends.

Today as an adult, nothing had changed. She was an outsider. She still came across many of the boys and girls she knew in school. They were all married now with two or three or even four children. They always exchanged warm greetings and shallow dialogue; *hola, qué onda?* how are you? how are the children? Nice to see you, *hasta luego.* They never invited her to their fiestas and piñata parties and the summer dances at the ranches, not from any lack of feeling but for lack of thought. What was Esperanza going to do at a fiesta? Sit and watch the others have a good time? No! It would be painful and humiliating to everyone. It was easier to go on with your life and forget Esperanza even existed. And because she was excommunicated from their lives Esperanza was never asked to be a godmother. She would never have that close relationship with a *comadre* or a *compadre* like all the others.

The miracle was that Esperanza was not embittered, never jealous of others. Her eyes always appeared to be smiling and her smile was there for everyone. She only expressed her resentment to herself when she was alone. It was at the sight of *novios* strolling arm in arm or sharing an ice cream, or a young mother with a tiny pink baby in her arms, that she felt left out of life. The feeling of being forgotten by God was an open wound on her soul.

She hobbled into the flower shop and ordered the extra roses from Doña Pilar. El Asustádo, Doña Pilar's teenage son with spiked hair, walked back with Esperanza carrying four cartons of roses in a hand truck. The boy thought he looked *padre* but he really looked more frightened than cool, hence the sobriquet. He told Esperanza he was saving up for a gold earring but Doña Pilar made it plain that the day he wore an earring she would send him to school in his sister's skirt. He put the flowers down for her and returned to his mother's flower shop. He would be back later in the evening to help Esperanza close up and carry everything back that didn't get sold.

By seven in the evening traffic was thinning out and all the street vendors began to close down their stalls and push their little carts toward home. The street musicians and performers were gone now, and the gay melancholy music of mariachis could be heard coming from the cafes and cantinas near the plaza. Esperanza did more business than she expected and was glad she had the extra roses. She began packing everything away. Soon El Asustádo would be here to carry everything back.

"*Hola, muchachita bonita!*"

It was Don Tibursio. He stood in front of Esperanza with his bright cumulus of colored balloons. "*Buenas noches*, Don Tibursio. Did you have a good day?"

"A very good day, *muchachita bonita*." He always called her "pretty little girl." "I earned tomorrow's tortillas. Now it is time to go home to my wife and a bowl of beans."

"Give my *saludos* to Doña Carmen."

"I will, I will." He handed Esperanza a red Mylar balloon in the shape of a heart swollen with helium and tied to a long thin red ribbon.

"Ay, Don Tibursio!" She tried to throw her arms around the old man but he was surrounded by too many balloons. She watched him wander off toward home. The dear old man's thoughtfulness brought a warm smile to Esperanza's pretty face.

She looked at the bright red heart tugging eagerly on the end of the ribbon, pulling at her hand like an impatient child. "What's your hurry, where are you going? If I let you go you will only wander forever and ever and get lost. I guess I'll just take you home and tether you to my bedpost."

The big bronze bells from the Church of Our Lady of Guadalupe began their imperative clanging, announcing eight o'clock Mass, each ringing note overlapping the next until the warm night resonated with a solemn dissonance.

And that's when the inspiration burst into flower.

Quickly Esperanza found a scrap of paper and a ballpoint pen in her purse. She dashed off a few lines, tied the note securely to the ribbon, then opened her hand and watched her heart climb high into the night and into the waiting arms of a thousand stars.

Then, like a ship swaying in heavy seas, Esperanza limped to the curb where Ernesto waited to help her into his blue and white taxi No. 12 for the trip home to her Nana.

II

Lic. Salvador Fuentes Enriquez emptied his bursting bladder behind the chicken house and, zipping up, returned to finish his work. He drove the last screw through the hinge on the gate, wiped his sweaty brow on his arm, and put down his tools. "Now how do I get all the chickens back in?" he asked himself. He could probably round them up with grain but first he'd better collect the eggs. The sensuous smell of meat and onions browning over a wood fire made his stomach growl, making a noise like he'd swallowed an angry cat. He inhaled every delicious molecule. The good smells were coming from his own kitchen, he was actually hungry for a good meal, and he wasn't crying. In fact, he was ravenous. A good sign.

Big improvement, he thought, maybe I'm finally making progress against the black tide of grief. Suddenly Claudia appeared through a window in his mind unbidden. If she could see me now, she'd laugh, he thought. The most prominent *licenciado* in Durango, a man who thought eggs came from cartons at the super market, playing ranchero in some desolate village in Baja California. But that's as far as the thought got when once again he realized he was thinking of Claudia and wasn't pushing back the tears. Then he felt the sting in his eyes and knew he'd allowed himself to get too close to the past. He bit down painfully on his finger to slay the thought while still in its infancy. He knew it was a bad habit. It began ten years ago. The pinkie of his left hand was covered with dark scar tissue, the nail permanently discolored. He headed toward the house. Pachita would be making those huge fluffy white tortillas the size of pillowcases. He'd worry about the eggs and the chickens later.

Pachita met him at the front door just as he stepped up on the porch. "I was just going to go looking for you, Don Chava." The dear old woman was short and round like a clay fireplace. She kept her hair, white as porcelain, tied back with a wide ribbon that usually clashed outrageously with the bright calico dusters she wore over black cotton leggings. Winter or summer she wore a knitted cardigan. Pachita was still in possession of most of her teeth, and had no need for glasses. She was old enough to be Salvador's mother so felt perfectly natural using the pet name common to all boys given the name of savior, provided she precede it with *Don* and spoke to him always as *Usted*. She went to the massive wood-burning stove and with two hands removed the enormous tortilla from the griddle and turned it over. "Everything will be ready by the time you wash up."

Salvador was only a few minutes and now sat before a large plate steaming with tender chunks of beef and potatoes smothered in dark chile colorado. A side dish held his favorite vegetable of tender, succulent cactus. He considered hiring Pachita five years ago the smartest thing he'd ever done. She came in every Thursday to clean his house, do his laundry, and cook the food he liked best. Salvador couldn't fry an egg. His culinary skills were limited to putting a slice of bread in the toaster and pouring corn flakes into a bowl. His biggest achievement was reheating the food she left for him.

Pachita put a chilled amber bottle of Tecate near his plate. "There is going to be a big fiesta in town Saturday night. I have your pretty yellow shirt all pressed for you."

The old woman was a treasure. She knew more about human nature than a clinical psychologist with a Ph.D in behavioral science, and never had to crack a book. Her credential was seventy-five years of life, raising eleven children of her own, and several grandchildren. She had decided that the time had come for the *licenciado* to leave his ten years of bitter widowhood behind him and begin to rejoin the living. If there was a down-side to Pachita it was that she saw it as her special mission in life to see that he was happily married once again to a nice girl who knew how to look after a man. Pachita believed all men needed looking after. Over the last five years in his employ she drew out little bits and pieces of his life until now she was convinced she knew what he needed better than he did. It wasn't long before she assumed the role of surrogate mother with gentle heart and firm hand.

"Oh, that's fine, Pachita," he said noncommitally around a forkful of cactus.

"You have to stop hiding away from life and go make yourself whole again."

Salvador had no interest in making the acquaintance of a "nice girl" and hadn't felt libidinous desires in years. He didn't have the courage to tell her he didn't want to hear it again, she spoke only what was in her dear old heart. "Too old."

"Oh, *sí*! Too old. Look at you. Fifty years old, the lean body of a bullfighter, an abundance of wavy black hair with little flecks of silver." She didn't go on to mention the deep golden eyes, the Pedro Infante mustache that would make any woman's loins shiver with passion. "I expect next week I will have to carry you into the bathroom." Pachita finished with a warm gurgling laughter, took another hot tortilla from the griddle and put it in the basket. "No, Don Chava, you have not earned the title *old*."

Salvador didn't take offense. He looked at the wrinkled hands that so lovingly tucked a hot tortilla in the basket, the brown face puckered like seersucker that gave the old woman a sage beauty. But Pachita was getting too close to the truth and he wasn't ready for Truth.

He could sum up his life in one sentence. Married Claudia at twenty-five, fifteen years later she died of cervical cancer, no children. *Fin.* At first he tried, he really tried to go through the ordeal of living, but everything in the house triggered a painful memory that wrenched his heart. Claudia was in every room. The big bed with her side empty every night was unbearable. He moved to the spare room. But that didn't work either. That's when he decided to erase the past from memory and go to some place he'd never heard of, where no one knew him and the past would no longer exist. After five years of emotional incontinence Salvador sold the house where he and Claudia had been so happy. The law firm he sold to his partners but kept the two apartment houses for income. He said goodbye to his aging parents, gave his Jetta to his sister, bought a Jeep Cherokee, and headed north as far from Durango as he could get. Day and night he drove like a *demónio* as though he could outrun grief. When and how he left the mainland and ended up in Baja California, he couldn't say. The whole trip was a blur. Now here he was in the Valley of Tanama, about twenty kilometers south of Tecate. He bought a few hectares with a modest adobe house with a red tile roof. There were only three rooms, but they were large and comfortable; a living room with a huge fireplace, a kitchen with a wood-burning range, his bedroom, and a small bathroom. If he left the kitchen door open the wood range could also heat his bedroom. The bathroom was an ice cave all year long.

The homestead was in the most desolate part of Tanama. His closest neighbors were trees. There were no memories here, nothing to remind him of Claudia, no ghosts, nothing to haunt him. He rarely left his little rancho except for a quick trip to a little grocery store that never had what he wanted or to the hardware store or to pay his light bill. He knew no one and no one came by. He would go a full week without hearing a human voice, with the exception of Pachita who walked almost two kilometers to come to work. If he felt like conversation he would talk to El Guardián, a big shaggy mongrel who was always at his side offering him friendship with big slurpy licks on his face, and Mariquita, a fluffly marmalade cat. La Cabrona, a mouse-colored jenny with cute long furry ears she loved to have scratched, didn't have a lot of conversation and she was quick to kick him in the *nalgas* if she was so disposed. He also looked after a flock of colored chickens and two obese geese. He kept himself busy from dawn until dark, growing corn and tomatoes, green and yellow squash, and a patch of strawberries he unwillingly shared with the rabbits. When he wasn't tending his crops or his animals he was gathering, hauling, and splitting firewood to meet the voracious demands of the fireplace and the kitchen stove. Long, hard days of arduous labor kept unwanted thoughts at bay. At night he would read translations of Oscar Wilde, Somerset Maugham, Proust, and the intimate life of Mozart by Wolfgang Hildesheimer. When he couldn't force his eyes to stay open he would fall into bed and pray he wouldn't wake up. Every day he told himself he had no reason to go on breathing. He kept no clock, no calendar, nothing that could remind of him of Claudia's birthday, their anniversary, or the festive holidays. Christmas was just another day. Music only stirred the ashes that smoldered in his heart. The music he and Claudia liked best now tore him apart. He had no television, no radio. When Pachita arrived early in the morning to start her work he assumed it was Thursday. He knew he'd made the right decision coming out here. He wasn't a happy man, but he wasn't looking for happiness. He came to find emotional solvency.

"I hope you go, Don. You need to get out among people again. It is not a good thing when your only friends are a dog and a cat."

"There's La Cabrona and the chickens and the geese."

Pachita's answer was a tsk! She stirred the kettle boiling on the stove that was rattling its lid and dribbling moisture on the hot iron surface with a hiss. She pulled the sleeves of her cardigan down over her hands as pot holders and slid the kettle to another burner. "I'm telling you this for your own good, Don."

His mother used to tell him the same thing. "I need some things from town anyway, so I probably will stop by and watch the festivities." He had no doubt Pachita knew perfectly well he was lying only to close the subject. You don't keep many secrets from the woman who for the last five years cleans your house, prepares your food, and washes and folds your underwear.

Two weeks later Salvador was standing waist-high in chaparral cutting kindling with a machete. The smells coming from the house told him lunch would soon be ready. It smelled like *machaca*. He could see Pachita walking between the rows of corn so he knew there would be fresh sweet corn on the cob dripping with butter for his customary afternoon snack. She always served it to him with a salt shaker, a little powdered chile, and a wedge of lemon. Not once today did his thoughts wander off to memories of the past. He felt he was improving.

"Mariquita, I almost beheaded you!" Salvador screamed. The marmalade cat leaped at something in the direct path of the machete just as he took a swing. Mariquita scampered away unimpressed and Salvador saw what had aroused the cat's curiosity and nearly cost her a life. Something red and shiny was fluttering in the chaparral. He reached in for it and pulled out a bright red heart balloon on a long red ribbon.

"What is that you've found?" Pachita called over.

"It looks like some child has lost her balloon."

They headed back toward the house together, Pachita with four ears of sweet corn cradled in her apron, Salvador carrying the balloon to put it in the trash bin up at the house. They stepped into the kitchen together. Pachita shucked the corn, removed the silk, and dropped the ears into the big boiling kettle with the smoky black bottom. Salvador dropped the balloon on his chair and went to get cleaned up. He was ravenous.

The balloon, now low on helium, bobbed at about the height of the table, dragging its long red ribbon on the floor. Pachita served what he hoped he'd smelled earlier, a big plate of *machaca* in eggs. She folded a fluffy white tortilla in the basket and brought him his chilled bottle of Tecate.

"The corn will be ready for you later."

"Where did you learn to make *machaca* like this?"

"In Sonora where *machaca* originated. In those days it was made from beef that hung out in a scorching sun to dry for several days."

"And these magnificent tortillas? Never saw anything like this in Durango."

Pachita checked the fire, placed another log in the firebox, and adjusted the damper. "Also in Sonora. My grandmother taught me when I was just a little thing. During the Revolution corn was scarce. The government took it all. Even the corn you grew yourself the soldiers would come and take it away. So they started making their tortillas with flour." She crossed to the table and grabbed the wayward balloon before it drew too close to the stove. She wound the ribbon around her wrist. "Did you see this, Don?"

"What?"

Pachita handed him the ribbon. "Didn't you notice? There appears to be a note tied to the ribbon."

"You're right." Salvador took the balloon from her and began to untangle the paper from the ribbon. The paper was badly creased and the writing smudged from morning dew but he unfolded it carefully, smoothed it out on his thigh, and read out loud.

"Dear God. *O glorioso omnipotente* Señor. I love You and appeal to Your infininite wisdom. I am twenty-six years old today and still unclaimed as a woman. I beg You bring me an *amigo salvador* to save me from my *desgrácia*. If You trust him, I will trust him. I ask this in the name of El Santo Padre, Jesus, y Espiritu Santo. Esperanza."

"How is it signed?"

"It's smudged here but it looks like it was simply signed *hope*."

"Let me look." Pachita took the note and studied the blots. "No, she spelled hope with a capital E, so Esperanza is her name. What are you going to do with it?"

"Nothing, of course. What is there for me to do?"

"A great deal! Comfort the poor girl for one thing, and help her with her burden if you can."

"Ay, Pachita! It is all very romantic but we don't even know who she is. She says 'save me from my *desgracia*' but we don't know what her misfortune might be."

"But, don't you see? It doesn't matter. This poor woman has asked God's help."

"Then it's for God to do."

"Forgive my *indiscreción*, Don, but have you thought that God didn't send it to Gomez the grocer, or Chemo the blacksmith, or to me, or to anyone else? She prayed for a *salvador* and your name is Salvador. God sent it to *you*."

Salvador sighed. He couldn't argue God's intentions.

Pachita thought she was overstepping her place with her employer, but she was so caught up in her passion she couldn't stop. "And you are too young to remain hidden in the cold darkness for the rest of your life. I have lived a long time, Don Chava, and after three-quarters of a century of life, I can tell you life isn't all sweet cakes. It also comes with onions to make us cry. But we go on."

She ladled the last spoonful of *machaca* on his plate and, using the sleeves of her cardigan again, slid the kettle of corn to a back burner where it would simmer slower. "You must get back out in the sunhine and let the sun warm you back to life, like spring gives new life to a tree that has been dead all winter." She pulled another tortilla off the hot griddle and put it in front of him. "Pardon my bold *confianza*, Don Chava, but for the last five years I've watched you torture yourself. You throw away the corn and eat the husks."

"And how do I go about finding her?"

"Begin looking at market, of course. Tecate is a small pueblo."

Salvador saw Pachita's discomfort and he didn't want to embarass her any more. "All right, I'll look into it during the week."

The following Thursday morning Pachita was already at her cast-iron stove stirring pots and stoking the fire when Salvador came in for breakfast. She poured him coffee and served him a large plate of scambled eggs and sausage with golden brown potatoes and a side of refried beans dusted with white *cotija* cheese. They chatted easily about the weather and other trivia of no consequence. The fact that the subject of the balloon and the prayer never came up in the conversation was sufficient for Pachita to know for a fact that her employer did not go to the aid of the desperate girl. She judiciously refrained from comment.

Salvador finished his huge breakfast and snatched a fresh tortilla from the basket as he went out to work.

By one o'clock in the afternoon Salvador had split a huge pile of eucalyptus logs, hoed the corn, and staked up tomato vines while

El Guardián and Mariquita watched. He was so exhausted he could hardly stand up but no vagrant thought of Claudia or the past came to haunt him, and that was his first and only objective for each day. He pulled off his battered straw hat and felt cool air where the hat had been. He wiped the sweat off his head and face with an old bandana, and began the long walk back to Pachita and the house. And a big hearty lunch. On the way he thought he would put the donkey back in her pen for the afternoon. But La Cabrona perceived his intentions and she was not pleased. As soon as he got close she spun around, kicked out with her hind legs, the sharp hooves just grazing his *nalgas*, then ran off across the field.

"*Cabrona!*"

When he came in all scrubbed Pachita was working over pots and kettles on the massive cast-iron range, turning things in a huge skillet that sizzled deliciously. As soon as Salvador sat down he was smearing butter on a fluffy hot tortilla. Pachita then put a big plate of fried corn husks in front of him and came back with his chilled bottle of Tecate just the way he liked it.

III

The following Sunday afternoon Salvador was strolling among the stalls at market.

"Ding-ding-a-ling! *Nieve de chocolate, mango, limón, y melón!*"

He motioned to the man singing his song behind the pushcart and was now enjoying the sweet, wet, cold fruity tang of a mango Popsicle. It was a challenge trying to keep the drips from his yellow shirt and light brown jeans. He wasn't even sure why he was doing this except to placate Pachita. He'd already walked the length of the street earlier. No one knew him and he knew no one. It would help if I knew who I was looking for, he thought. I wonder what she looks like? Is she fat as a goose? Is she fair as the wild lilacs that carpet the hills of Tanama in the spring? Or dark, maybe, dark as the polished russet of the manzanita tree?

"*Tamales...tamales calientes*, señor? We have beef, pork, cheese, and corn!""

"Iguana on a stick, señor?"

He watched the Sunday crowds. Men, women, families walking with their children. Sometimes three generations strolled together, the youngest child straddling his father's neck, little hands gripping his hair. A handsome youth walked past him with his pretty *novia*, their arms encircling each other's waist. Salvador remembered when he and Cla— no! Turn off the memory! From somewhere behind him he heard a violin in the company of a guitar playing a love song that was vaguely familiar. He could hum the melody line along with the violin but the lyrics were gone. He could feel the friendly sun smiling on his back. It felt good to hear voices, music, talk to people, even if only street vendors. As he negotiated his melting mango ice he began to realize that the long years of self-imposed exile, the loneliness, were becoming unbearable. Maybe it *was* time to let the sunshine back into his life.

"Shine, señor, shine?" The youthful soprano cut off his moment of self-communion. A young boy in stained blue jeans and Chargers T-shirt stood in front of him, a shoeshine box slung over one shoulder, a folding chair under his arm. He pointed an accusatory finger at Salvador's dusty dress boots.

Salvador looked down at his footwear and decided it was hardly an option. He took the chair the boy unfolded and put his right foot up on the box. While the boy went to work Salvador decided to gather information.

"I suppose you know everyone here in the pueblo."

"*Sí*, señor. I have been working here at market since I was eight years old."

"How old are you now?"

"Twelve, señor."

Salvador was impressed with the neatness of the boy and the absence of ear hoops, nose rings, gelled hair or other affectations that floated into Tecate from American television. And it didn't escape his notice that the boy had impeccable manners. Not a single sentence came out of his mouth without the honorific señor. He decided he might as well get to the point and take a shot in the dark. "Do you know anyone here named Esperanza?"

"*Sí*, señor. She is the señorita who sells flowers over there." He tossed his head in the direction of a mountain of watermelon.

"*Listo*, señor!" The little gentleman said when he was finished.

Salvador reached in his pocket and gave the boy two ten-peso coins.

"Forgive me, señor, it is twenty-four pesos."

"Twenty-four?" He reached into his pocket again to dig out four more small coins.

"*Sí*, señor, our currency has gone to *la chingada* in the last few weeks. Now I have to pay more for my supplies, señor."

Laughing at the incongruity, Salvador slipped the young bottomliner an additional five pesos and began another stroll through the market crowds. He headed in the direction of the watermelons but at a distance from the shopkeepers so as not to be noticed. It would feel good to talk to a pretty girl once again, he told himself. He found the flower stall and the thought perished when he saw the orangutan who sold the flowers. His heart dropped. She was definitely in her twenties, dressed in a pair of gray sweatpants that fitted her like the loose skin on the hindquarters of a hippopotamus. A voluminous white blouse worn on the outside hid a backside bigger than La Cabrona's.

There were no illusions here. Might as well get it over with, he thought. I'll meet her, talk to her for a while, say *adios*, and I can honestly tell Pachita I did my part.

"*Buenas tardes*, you are Esperanza?"

The orangutan smiled graciously and laughed. "No, señor, I am not Esperanza. I am watching her place while she goes to the you-know-where." She laughed again. "Would you like a dozen fresh roses to delight your señora? Or perhaps to atone?"

Of course, he thought, what else would a fifty-year old codger want with flowers? He felt his age and then some. "To atone," he said, not sure why. "I'll come back and pick them up after I've had something to eat."

As it turned out, he didn't lie. He bought an ear of sweet corn on the cob dusted with chili powder and dripping with butter and lemon. When he deposited the cob in a trash barrel and wiped his hands and mouth with the wilted napkin provided, he decided to make one last journey to the flower girl if only to have an honest report to make to Pachita.

Salvador came to the flower stall and froze at the apparition before him. There, in living flesh stood Renoir's "Young Woman With Flowers." He was mesmerized. Awestruck. She was surrounded by flowers just like the color plate in the book of Impressionists he had at home. She was wrapping bouquets of roses in plastic wrap. The artist had dressed her in a cheery fuchsia summer frock that celebrated the contours of womanhood and enhanced her tiny waist. The Renoir scene was splashed with dapples of sunlight that filtered through the trees above. Hair of ebon hue flowed in shimmering waves to the small of her back, her skin was smooth as damask, and when she turned her eyes on him, he could hear the first line of *Aquellos Ojos Verdes,* Those Green Eyes, in his head. Then, when her mouth blossomed into a smile, the voltage was too great for him and he could feel his heart overheating.

Salvador came up to her. "*Buenas tardes,* are you — are you Esperanza?"

"*Sí.* Were you wanting a nice arrangement?" She had a voice like champagne. "I can make up a very charming bouquet of pink and red roses nestled in fern."

"Well, actually, I — I didn't really come for flowers."

"You didn't?" Her champagne voice lost some of its bubbles.

"No, you see, I uh," he stammered like a schoolboy, "I uh, found your heart — I mean your balloon!"

Renoir's Young Woman With Flowers covered her face with both hands.

"I'm sorry, I haven't introduced myself. I'm Salvador Fuentes Enriquez, your *servidor.*"

It took Esperanza a moment to make the connection. Salvador! she screamed in thought. She looked into a smooth caramel face that reminded her of chamois cloth. There was a definite sadness in those deep dark eyes, so brown, they looked almost golden. "You — you — you mean, you're the *salvador?*" She stopped before she said, "did God send you?" and took his offered hand. "And I am Esperanza Contreras, *servidora.*"

Neither spoke, neither moved. They just stood for long moments joined by two hands that showed no inclination to part. Esperanza was first to release his hand, and taking out her little white handkerchief, dampened it in fresh clean water and began to sponge off the front of his shirt. "You've been eating mango and the syrup they use in those ices stains if you don't get it off immediately. And such a pretty shirt too." She inserted her free hand between two buttons to support the fabric while she worked vigorously on the stain. She could feel his warm bare skin on the back of her hand. She kept her eyes on her work but had already surveyed that beautiful doeskin face and kissable mouth.

Salvador watched her hands. The simple human touch, a warm hand on his naked skin, sent a spark all the way down his spine.

In a few circular strokes it was gone. "There!"

"Clean shirt, clean soul!" My God, I haven't tossed out flowery *pirópos* in years. "*Gracias.*"

Her laughter sounded like little silver chimes. "So, where was it you found my pray — my balloon?"

"In Tanama."

"Way out there? That's amazing. No wonder it took so long." Now, why did I say that? He'll think I was counting the days.

They both felt awkward now, just looking at each other, then Esperanza began to feel she was standing in front of him without her clothes. This gorgeous man read my intimate message to God. He knows my age, he knows how desperate I am, he knows everything.

Salvador recovered first. "Maybe I could come by later and we can take a little walk around the plaza. Would you like that?"

"No! I mean, I'm so busy." Now, that was stupid, she scolded herself, why did I say that? It's exactly what I want. But I can't possibly go for a walk with him. That would ruin everything!

Salvador perceived her unease. "Or if you prefer, we could go somewhere for dinner." He didn't wait for an answer. "When do you finish here?"

"I'll close at eight tonight."

"And where's a good place?"

"La Fonda on the other side of the plaza has very good food."

"*Magnífico*! I have some errands to do. I'll be back for you at eight."

Salvador arrived at the flower stand just as the steam whistle at the Tecate Brewery blasted the tranquil evening to announce twenty hundred hours.

She wasn't there.

Well, why is it I'm not surprised? Did I disappoint her? Was she just trying to get rid of me in a nice way? Okay, he thought, I didn't really expect anything else. I really didn't want to come here in the first place. I can tell Pachita I made an honest try. He turned to go.

"*Perdon* señor, are you Salvador?"

Salvador turned to see a teenager he hadn't noticed before. His hair stood in long stiff spikes that put Salvador in mind of the yucca that grew wild on his ranch. He was loading cartons of flowers onto a hand truck. "*Sí*, I am Salvador."

"Señorita Esperanza said to tell you she would meet you at La Fonda."

The short sentence restored his spirits like a tonic. He was on his way to La Fonda with a smile he was helpless to contain. To dinner. To dinner with a pretty girl!

He was caught in a delicious web of wonderful smells the minute he walked in the door. Mariachis were melting hearts at a table at the back. He saw her immediately in her fuchsia dress sitting at a corner table covered with a white cloth. She was holding a menu.

"I thought it would be best to come in and hold a table." She smiled up at him. "Sometimes you can't get in at all."

"Good idea!" He took the seat facing her. She didn't look like she had worked all day in her crisp summer dress. It had a fascinating scooped neck, but he didn't want to get caught looking. He kept his eyes on hers.

The man sitting in front of her reminded Esperanza of Pedro Infante, that handsome *charro* she'd seen in old movies when her Nana took her to the Cine Tecate when she was a girl. His soft mouth appeared to be made of a darker velvet. It was an effort not to reach out and touch it with her fingers.

Both were relieved when Beto, the waiter, came up and mutual assessment ceased. "*Hola*, Esperanza! *Buenas noches*, señor. A drink before you order?"

"*Hola*, Beto. *Sí*, una margarita."

"The same for me," Salvador said.

Both were too shy to initiate conversation. They talked with their eyes until Beto returned with two margaritas.

"*Salud*."

"*Salud*."

"Just the thing I needed."

"Me too."

"I was just thinking," she began tentatively.

"What?"

"Well, that your name is savior and my name is hope. Isn't that extraordinary?"

"Yes! I was thinking the very same thing."

"How did you ever find my message in Tanama?"

"I was out cutting firewood and I found it hanging in the branches."

"You're a rancher?"

"No," he laughed. "A lawyer."

"You're not from here are you?"

"Durango. How could you tell?"

"I've never seen you before and there are no strangers in Tecate."

"What about you?" he asked before she could ask any more questions.

"Born and raised right here in Tecate by my Nana who was my mother and father and because I never had a *madrina*, she was also my godmother." She took a long sip of her margarita. "She's also my best friend."

"How fortunate for you to have her. How fortunate for her that you know it. One day I will have to meet this incredible woman."

What do I say now? I think I've already said too much, she admonished in thought. She had lots of questions; was he married, divorced, single? Or was he just another macho adventurer? She wasn't ready to investigate. That would only give him license to glean information she wasn't ready to reveal. "Do you have farm animals?"

"Not many. The usual chickens, a dog and a cat. And La Cabrona."

"La Cabrona!" she laughed, "who is she, your wife?" She wanted to bite her tongue but the words were already out of her mouth.

The evening would be ruined if he went into explanations. "A donkey."

"A donkey! And why does she have such an evil name?"

"Fits her personality."

"A big red rooster to summon the morning?"

"Four."

"What a chorus that must be! I'd love to see it one day."

"I'll bring you out anytime you want."

Esperanza realized she had just dug herself into a trap with no way out. She tried to take refuge in her margarita but there was nothing left but foam. Fortunately, Beto was standing at their table to bail her out.

"Ready to order?"

"Bring me the *chiles rellenos*, Beto."

"I'll have the steak ranchero. But you might as well refill the margaritas." Salvador looked to Esperanza for approval. She nodded.

It is just as well that neither the grieving Salvador nor the lonely Esperanza could read minds. Salvador strained to control his emotions. *Don't get too excited. This is all very nice but no gorgeous twenty-six year old girl wants anything to do with a man old enough to be her father and in the Indian summer of his life.* Similar thoughts came to Esperanza. *Be realistic. Is a man going to date a girl with a deformity? A man wants a girl he can take for walks, go to dances, have fun with — not some cripple!*

Presently Beto put their food in front of them and retreated. They quickly fell to the pleasant task before them. With the speed and safety of thought, Salvador admitted he was feeling emotions he hadn't allowed himself to feel. Despite ten years of loyal and faithful mourning, Esperanza's youthful beauty and innocent aura of sexuality pulled at his heart. *I feel like I've been dead and the beautiful girl in front of me is breathing life into me.* A red light flashed in his mind. *If she perceives I'm interested in her in any romantic sense it'll scare her off. But maybe there is a way I can could help her. But how? She mentions the need for a* salvador *to overcome her* desgrácia. *But she gives no indication what that misfortune might be. I can't very well ask. It will have to come from her. When she's ready.* He looked up at his dinner date.

"How are the *chiles rellenos*?"

"*Ricos!* How is your steak ranchero?"

"*Delicioso!*"

Esperanza was enjoying the dinner and the company but while she tried to make small talk a lot was racing through her mind. *What do I do now? If I reveal my feelings, if I confess that I'm already unredeemably in love with him, I'll lose him. The minute he sees me walk he'll feel he was deceived. Cheated. No man can forgive that.*

"Is everything all right?" Beto asked. Seeing empty plates he began to gather them up. "And what shall it be for dessert? We are famous for our flan."

"Oh, not for me, Beto."

"I can never pass up a good flan," Salvador said.

"And of course, coffee for you both, *sí*?"

Beto was back in minutes with two coffees and one beautiful flan.

Esperanza took the dessert fork from the table, scooped up a little piece and ate it with eyes closed in ecstacy. "Mmm! You're going to love it." She took another piece and fed it to Salvador.

"This is fantastic flan! We have to do this again."

"Anytime."

Her answer encouraged him. "Oh, did you see the poster in the plaza? An evening of country dances."

Esperanza panicked. A dance! "I'm afraid I can't. I uh, I uh," she stammered and felt her cheeks flush.

"*Magnífico!*"

"What?"

"I was terrified you'd say yes," he laughed. He laid his hands over both of hers. "You see," he said, leaning toward her with a conspiratorial whisper, "I can't dance." That brought him a beautiful laugh. "It's a problem with my feet. My left foot and my right foot can't seem to come to an agreement with the music."

Esperanza slipped her hands over his and squeezed. They were thus engaged when she saw her old girlfriend Helena Peñalosa leaving with her husband on her arm. Helena was so busy staring at them her mouth hung open and she rear-ended a busboy with a huge clatter of falling dishes and silverware. It brought Esperanza a secret smile.

Salvador made a subtle sign to the mariachis and Esperanza was surrounded by two guitars, guitarron, three violins and a silvery trumpet. They were dressed in tight black pants with silver conchos glimmering down the sides, black jackets with silver piping, and white shirts with a broad red ribbon recklessly knotted at the neck. The dashing tall man on trumpet looked at Salvador for his request.

"*Aquellos Ojos Verdes*," he said, and the old song, an ode to pretty girls with green eyes, filled La Fonda from walls to smoky ceiling. They held hands across the table while that emotion that only those who have heard mariachis can understand, swept over both hope and savior. Little drops of happy tears clung to Esperanza's long dark lashes when she realized she was actually on a real date for the first time in her life! Salvador felt a surge in the area of his heart akin to pain, and started to bring his little finger to his mouth then quickly controlled the reflex. Would the past haunt him forever?

But the vulnerable moment passed unnoticed and he succeeded in making his escape from old ghosts. It became an evening of romance and magic for them both. "Same time next week?" Salvador asked when the mariachis were summoned to another table.

"I would love it!"

"I don't want this to end but I suppose I'd better be taking you home." Salvador called Beto, settled the check, and walked around the table to Esperanza.

"Oh! I left my shawl hanging over a chair at the flower stand."

"Stay here, I'll bring it."

Salvador found the flower stand deserted. The only thing there was a card table and folding chair with a white shawl draped over the back. When he walked back into La Fonda Beto was clearing the table and Esperanza was nowhere in sight. She probably went off to the you-know-where, he thought, when Beto spoke up. "Señorita Esperanza just left. Her grandmother sent a taxi for her."

"I have her shawl."

"You can leave it with me. I'll give it to her when she comes in tomorrow."

They exchanged thank yous and *buenas noches* and Salvador walked across the deserted plaza with the strains of *Aquellos Ojos Verdes* still playing in his head. He may have missed the opportunity to kiss her good night, but he had a date with hope for the same time next week.

IV

Thump-thumpa-thump!
Bamba, Bamba!
Yo no soy marinéro
por ti seré, por ti seré
Bamba, bamba!

When Salvador stepped into La Fonda he thought he'd walked in on a Zapatista rebellion set to music. He took a step back to take in the chaos. Men and women, the young, the old, the locals, the gringos, abandoned their dinners and were now hopping and stomping to the infectious beat of *La Bamba*. An American woman, high on margaritas and mariachis, threw herself in front of Beto without missing a beat. Salvador smiled to himself as he watched poor Beto join her stomp for stomp, hop for hop, for about two measures then escape to the kitchen to pick up an order.

He scanned the scene through the smoke and found Esperanza seated at what they now considered to be "their table."

"You're the only one not in step with the insurgents," he shouted, touching his cheek to hers, as he sat in front of her. They could hardly hear each other talk. She smiled her reply.

They reached across the table for each other's hands until the final *thump!* ended the insurrection and La Fonda resumed its normal din for a Sunday evening. This was their sixth date. They had fallen into a comfortable routine. Esperanza arranged to come a little early and hold a table and thus spare Salvador the need to go first to the flower stand. He also accepted the fact that she always declined a stroll around the plaza. They said good night at their table. Maybe she was afraid of the dark. Of him? He didn't press it. What he didn't know was that as soon as he was out the door, Beto would escort her to the rear door where Ernesto waited for her in his blue and white taxi No.12.

Esperanza looked like she'd just climbed down from the sky in a summer shift of lavender blue, sleeveless and cut low. It was an effort not to stare. "How was your day?" he asked now that they could hear each other again.

"Very busy. I sold almost everything I had. How was your week at the rancho?"

"The usual routine, feed the chickens, hoe the corn, tend to the tomatoes, gather firewood, and avoid getting kicked in the *nalgas* by La Cabrona." He heard Esperanza's delicious laugh again.

"*Buenas noches*," Beto stood at their table and unloaded two margaritas from his tray. He knew their routine.

"You were *formidáble* on the dance floor, Beto, maybe you should take it up full time," Esperanza teased.

"That woman is here every weekend. You should have seen me *last* night!" Beto laughed. "I"ll leave you two alone to relax and enjoy your drinks for a while."

"*Salud.*"

"*Provecho.*"

Now that the mariachis moved on to more romantic music, they chatted comfortably about everything but themselves. Salvador was enjoying his time with her and he didn't want to ruin it by rushing her. They still had not exchanged a real kiss, just a touching of the cheeks when he arrived and another when they said good night.

Two margaritas later Beto brought them a dinner of carne asada for Esperanza and the lobster plate for Salvador. They advanced on dinner with appetite. When it was time for dessert Beto brought them coffee and one flan, then watched with a smile while Esperanza fed him.

Seismologists at the Observatório de San Pedro Mártir claim that mariachis can pick up the vibrations emitted by a man and a woman in love through the strings of their violins. Tonight the mariachis confirmed that theory. They now gathered around Salvador and Esperanza, violins scribbling partial melodies, guitars forming chords. The only one not decorating the air with notes was the trumpet player because he was the spokesman. "A song? Something *alegre*, something *romántico*? Something to make you happy, something to make you weep? We can do all that in one song."

Salvador took Esperanza's hand that rested on the table. "You choose tonight." He didn't add *mi amor*, but the unspoken endearment hung in the air in front of them.

Esperanza clasped her hands to her bosom. "Would you remember *Viva Mi Desgrácia?*"

"Do I remember it? With tears in my eyes, señorita!" the man on trumpet answered. "Pedro Infante immortalized it." He gave the downbeat with the bell of his horn. And Mexico's most romantic waltz, a waltz written by Francisco Cardenas, the Strauss of Mexico, nearly a hundred years ago that can still summon tears, touched every heart in La Fonda.

Esperanza seemed to have left the real world of cakes and onions and stepped on to the dance floor in a frothy tangerine dress with a full skirt. She was in Salvador's arms, gliding, turning, moving as one across the floor to the evocative three quarter pulse. When the waltz reached the accelerando they were spinning across the floor, her tangerine skirt flaring open like a parasol in summer. She wrapped herself in music and drifted away into a waking dream. She was in love. She dreamed of Salvador every night. They kissed, they touched, they made love. When she woke her pillow was wet and she was alone. Then she sighed over the imaginary loss.

No one is immune to the sorcery of mariachis. Salvador too, was in another time zone, looking into the sweet laughing face of a beautiful ghost from his past. She was in his arms, dressed in a long gown of pink froth. By sheer force of will Salvador fought his way back to La Fonda and Esperanza.

Near the end of the waltz Esperanza returned to reality and looked over at the man she loved and would soon lose. Esperanza was immersed in that euphoria that comes to a woman in love. But the voice of her conscience nagged at her that it was time to come clean with Salvador. Every week she vowed to end the charade. But then the minute he came in and pressed his cheek to hers, all resolve crumbled and she told herself she would do it next time. She felt fraudulent. She held his golden eyes with her own until the last note of *Viva Mi Desgrácia* died in the smoky air.

For a long moment neither could form words. Their hands found each other across the table. Salvador was having trouble keeping his eyes above the neckline of her sky-blue dress and the little gold cross that rested on gentle swells. The thought came to him that he hadn't fallen asleep with his arms around someone in ten years and was somewhat startled when he became aware of a pleasant quiver somewhere in his loins. He was sure that part of him was dead then realized that physical desire couldn't get past the pain.

Esperanza held his hands tighter. She was in love at great risk to her heart.

Drinks, dinner, and dessert were over. They toyed with their coffee. Neither wanted to leave. Salvador lived for the weekend, he felt buoyant and alive for the first time in ten bitter years. The music he heard at La Fonda ran through his head all week, and he went about his work singing along with non-existent mariachis.

Esperanza too was transformed. She sang around the house. Her laughing smile never left her face. When Salvador placed his warm hands over her own, her deformity ceased to exist.

Reluctantly, Salvador signaled Beto for the check and excused himself.

"Wait for me. I'm just going to the you-know-where. I'll be right back to settle up the check with Beto."

"I'll be here."

When Salvador returned to their table Esperanza wasn't there. He assumed she was off on a similar errand and sat down to wait. Beto arrived with the check. He took the bills and went off to the cashier. He returned to Salvador, gave him his change and *gracias* for the generous tip. Esperanza still hadn't returned.

"And Esperanza?"

"Oh, she said there was a full moon tonight and it was too beautiful to be indoors. She told me to tell you to join her in the plaza."

Maybe it was true that Salvador couldn't dance. But right now he could have climbed up on the table and danced *La Bamba* with or without a partner. His heart swelled almost painfully with expectation. At last, a stroll in the plaza! Arm in arm under a full moon. And maybe, just maybe, a kiss under the stars. He bolted for the door.

The night was warm, sensual, scented with the perfume of sleeping tea roses and jasmine and wet grass. The moon, gowned in silver lamé, cast a magic spell over the plaza. If one of the old masters had painted Venus in Moonlight, Salvador was looking at her now, seated on a lacy wrought iron bench near the monument to Benito Juarez. Her blue summer dress was now washed in antique pewter. Her damask face, her smooth bare arms, and the slightest hint of cleavage, were cast in molten silver.

Wordlessly, the man who feared the past settled in beside the woman who feared the future. Her scent was elusive, erotic, a mysterious aura of roses and gardenias and lavender. The fragrance triggered a vague and distant memory and Salvador was helpless to stem the tears that now filled his eyes and threatened to spill down his face. He put one arm around her shoulder. Their mouths had yet to meet. Esperanza pressed her cheek to his and felt the warm wetness on his face.

They sat bathed in silver light. They were silent. Both had things to say. It was a long while before Salvador spoke and it wasn't what he intended to say. "Do you realize I have never seen you by moonlight? You're exquisite!"

Esperanza cradled his face in both hands. "And do you realize we hardly know each other? Who are we?"

"I can recite my entire life in three words. Wedded, widowed, childless." He put both his arms around her and pressed her to him. "And I love you, *mi amor.* I want to marry you."

"And what do you know about me? Nothing."

"I know all I have to know."

"Oh Salvador, Salvador!" She burst into tears.

"What is it, *mi amor,* what's wrong?"

Esperanza came out of his embrace so she could face him. "I love you, Salvador, I love you and I can't — I can't marry you!" she stammered through her sobs.

He held her wet face between his two hands. "And why not?" He wanted to make her smile, to stop her tears. "Is it my age? Do I remind you of your grandfather? Or maybe it's the face. Yes, the face! It would frighten our children. No, of course! It's my breath. Yes, that's it, my rancid breath that can wilt all your pretty roses with a single sigh!"

Tears and laughter came together in a flood. Then Esperanza stood. Salvador couldn't take his eyes off Venus in Moonlight.

Then Esperanza walked away from him, lurching and tilting and clumping with that hideous limp until she reached the steps of the kiosk. She stopped. Then turned to face him.

"Now you know me."

Salvador was up and had her tight in his arms in an instant. She wept bitterly. "This is what God made me!" she sobbed.

"*Mi amor, mi amor,* my darling Esperanza. Can you possibly believe I fell in love with your feet, your hands? Your nose? Your ears, maybe your liver? No, *mi amor,* I fell in love with *you!*" He wrapped her tighter in his arms. Esperanza swallowed salty tears. "We are more than a foot or a face. We are a heart and a soul. God doesn't make mistakes, *mi amor.* The only deformity that exists in nature is in the human mind."

He held her tighter to him. "Now, dry your tears, and say you'll marry me and forever be my *esperanza.*"

"And you, *mi amor,* will always be my *salvador.*"

Their lips came together for the first time.

"And now, my love. Once around the plaza?" He put out his arm.

Esperanza put her arm through his, and for the first time in her life, Esperanza Contreras, the crippled flower girl, strolled around the plaza in the moonlight with her *novio* on her arm.

Saturday

*L*ucrecia Martinez bowed her head before the ceramic figurine of Mary Magdalene that stood on top of the long-dead Kelvinator. "Your sins are my sins," she whispered. "And yet Jesus cleansed you of your sins and appeared before you after His resurrection." She anointed the little figure's feet with scented oil then wiped them with her hair just as Mary Magdalene had done for Jesus on the cross. "You were a woman of strength in a hostile world. Help me to be strong." Lucrecia lit a candle to her and came out to the front porch.

It was Saturday.

The air was thick with dirt, you could taste it, the heat too heavy to breathe without singeing the lungs. The summer rains never came this year. Just yesterday, dark virile clouds hung low. They came swaggering in all boast and bluster, flirting with mother earth, pledging rain and summer flowers. But it was all a puff-and-blow act. The fickle clouds soon broke their promise and wandered off to answer someone else's prayers.

Lucrecia took her Saturday place on the front steps of her little red brick house, unpainted, unfinished, unfulfilled. It consisted of two rooms where Lucrecia and her four kids lived, slept, ate. A blue plastic tarp anchored to the roof with rocks kept most of the rain out of the house when there was any. Electric power had been cut off for lack of funds sometime in the forgotten past when more critical needs had to be addressed. Like groceries.

She caught a whiff of her own scent; fresh lilacs, in her hair still damp from the bath, on her golden arms, on her Saturday dress, a bright yellow sundress with bare shoulders spattered with huge orange sunflowers. She wore her white plastic Saturday sandals.

Rrr- rrr- rrrr-rrrr.

Lucrecia watched little four-year old Betito playing in the dirt on his hands and knees with his little toy car while he provided various motor noises depending on engine load and road conditions. She looked out into the dirt road that ran in front of her house, a quagmire of red mud in the winter that often sucked a car under to the axles, in the dry season a deep river of brown dust powdery as baby talcum that coated everything outdoors and indoors. The grit could get between the sheets with you, in your eyes and mouth, even in your food. Lucrecia listened for the sound of a car.

Nothing.

Even in a small pueblo like Tecate where time is redundant, Lucrecia didn't need clock or calendar to know it was noon on Saturday. She heard the distant whistle of the passenger train from San Diego as it chugged into Tecate to unload a crowd of carefree Americans eager for a frosty margarita and the gay music of mariachis. It was a Saturday sound. The reverent strains of Ave Maria came floating on the warm air over every radio station in the nation precisely at noon. The street in front of her house was deserted. A couple of parked cars, the carcass of a black pickup across the street that had one less wheel than it had yesterday and fresh graffiti. Everyone in the *colonia* was sitting down to their heavy Saturday meal. She could hear Don Prudencio singing his madrigal several minutes before he came into view, consistent with Saturday convention.

"*Pan dulce!*" he sang to any housewife who might be within earshot. The long saddle-leather face cracked into a smile when he recognized Lucrecia sitting out front. A hand waved like a magician's wand without disturbing the balance of a tray laden with sweet bread balanced on his head. "*Pan dulce...cuatro por diez...cuatro por diez!*"

Again, Lucrecia scanned the dirt road as though some miracle that would solve all her problems would materialize from out of the brown dust. She could smell spicy sausage and beans and the unmistakable smell of pork simmering in jalapeño chiles with onions and cilantro. Somewhere in all the houses in the *colonia* the women would now be stirring pans that sizzled and hissed with good things to eat. They would lift the lids off bubbling kettles to inspect long yellow ears of fresh sweet corn that sent up a fragrant puff of white steam. The men would all be sitting around with a cold beer waiting to be called to the lunch table.

She waited.

A dusty Jeep Cherokee rumbled by. It was her neighbor Hortencia. She must have gone back to the store for something. She cast a look toward Lucrecia who raised her hand in greeting. Hortencia did not wave back. The look on the woman's face was an indictment.

No car yet. But she knew there was still time. It was still early. She spoke to Mary Magdalene half out loud, half to herself. "You too were a single mother. You birthed in adulterous bed. You suffered what I now suffer. You would understand." Over the years it was only the Holy Spirit of Mary Magdalene dwelling in her heart that she could count on for comfort and help. All she ever asked of her chosen patron was that she would give her of her strength, just enough to help her make it through the week. That's all. She never asked for more. And Mary Magdalene never failed her. Never.

Rrr-rrr-rrrr-rrrr.

Lucrecia tended a fertile garden of toxic weeds rooted in her memory and the instant she began her vigil on the front steps she drifted off into her usual Saturday thoughts; twenty-nine years old, four kids, no husband. No *novio.* No means of support. Why was I ever born a woman? To meet the needs of a man, bring children into life then depend on some *cabron* to feed me and his own children? Then watch the innocents suffer along with me? I gave my heart, my body, and my soul in exchange for betrayal. And now, there's nobody to see that they're fed and clothed.

Except me. It may have been July on the calendar but it was still February in Lucrecia's soul. When she went to her mother after her first disaster her mother would say, "That's real life, *mi amor.* Men play the maracas and we learn to dance to their rhythm." Well, dancing lessons are over for me! She never knew her father but her mother supplied a steady stream of stepfathers who were overly eager to know her. Love and security at home were an unknown experience in her young life.

Innocent of vanity and conceit, she knew she was, at twenty-nine, still attractive. Light still flickered in her large dark eyes, her skin, the color of comb honey, was soft and smooth and glossy as polished alabaster. In spite of having given light to four children, she was aware that the planes and curves of her body were still the target of men's eyes when she traversed the plaza on her way to market.

In mind-travel it only required microseconds to go back fourteen years in time when she was young and virginal, eager to experience life. At fifteen she had her full height and all her womanly contours. With eyes wide open an uninvited image of Concepcion took form, beautiful of face, skin the color of baked adobe, black curls, and dark laughing eyes that touched her everywhere.

She first met Concepcion at a dance at El Taconazo. A nice boy, twenty, *simpático*, tall, dark, and he could make her feel good all over. He crackled with macho energy and those *machismo* vibrations drew Lucrecia in like a magnet. He laughed in life's face and his love affair with alcohol was part of his charm. She was only fifteen and like a stray kitten, her young heart was vulnerable to any offer of shelter and kindness. And Concepcion was kind and generous. And he was so worldly! She'd never been out of Mexico, never even out of Baja California. Concepcion could thrill her for hours with all his tales of his adventures when he worked in the United States. Innocent, curious, and in love for the first time in her young life, Lucrecia dropped out of school to have her baby. Father Ruben baptized her Carmen. Concepcion was a bricklayer by trade. He built the little house where she now sat. Eighteen months later, came Magali. She was just learning to say mamá and papá when Papá crawled through the fence and went to the Other Side.

"Our family is growing and we need more money than I can make here," he told her. "I want you to have the best of everything, *mi amor.* On the Other Side I can make in a day what I earn here in a week."

"I would worry about you. Every day it gets more dangerous."

"El Gordo is going with me. We can look after each other. You have nothing to worry about, *corazón.*" He made love to her and promised to send a money order every week and that he would be home soon with bags of American dollars.

She never saw Concepcion again.

Was he dead, was he alive? Was he injured? The weeks of not knowing were driving her mad. He had to be dead. He'd never leave her stranded, penniless with two children. Never! Lucrecia went into mourning. Every day she walked to the *parroquia* to light a candle for him and place it before the Blessed Virgin. She left the little ones with a neighbor friend and cleaned other people's houses for grocery money. Nearly two years later El Gordo made it back home with the help of the U.S. Border Patrol and the rumor swept through Tecate like a Santa Ana wind: Concepcion was living with some girl up in Bakersfield. *I was abandoned like an unwanted cat with her litter of kittens.* Anger unfrocked grief.

Lucrecia wasted no time lamenting. She immediately found work doing the only thing she was qualified to do. She got a job sweeping the floors in an American cigar box factory. That's where she met Alfredo. She could see Alfredo was a party boy. All the girls in the factory were crazy for him. He flirted outrageously and dated all of them. But in her eyes, Alfredo was the Blue Prince; he worked hard, saved his money, and *he didn't drink.* He began by walking her home. She would serve him coffee. He played games with the little girls. And he bought all the groceries. Lucrecia made him *chiles rellenos* with rice and beans and went to the trouble of making flour tortillas from scratch. Alfredo thanked her and kissed her. Two kisses later she let him have the other half of her sofa bed.

Pilar was born nine months after the chile rellenos. Lucrecia quit her job to become a full-time mother and wife. She was good at both. She made a comfortable home for Alfredo and she waited upon his every whim like a handmaiden. He was a happy young man; he had a comfortable home, he came straight home after work and sat down to superb meals, and whenever he was so inclined, there was a gorgeous girl to play with him and a perfect body for him to play with. He looked like a man who had it all. Lucrecia had never felt such a sense of security before. Once again Lucrecia had shelter and kindness.

But in a few months Alfredo began to show signs of restlessness. He stayed out late and wandered off on weekends. He began to think of all the parties and the pretty girls out there. He was missing all the fun and decided he was saddled with more family than he wanted.

Lucrecia was alone again.

A few days after Alfredo was gone she realized she had a serious problem. Two girls age four and three, baby Pilar, and no way to feed them. She would go back to work. She could place Carmen and Magali in the *guardería* but there was no one to look after the baby. She went back to her neighbor to make the arrangements but her friend had moved away. Leaving the baby with her mother was out of the question while her latest pervert was in the house.

She would find work, at least part time, just to keep food on the table. She could work in the mornings while the two older ones were in the *guardería*. She immediately got work cleaning houses. But she had to bring baby Pilar with her. There was no place to put her while she worked. This arrangement did not appeal to the señoras she worked for, and in a short time, there was no work for her.

Fortunately, Lucrecia was a thrifty girl who held on to every coin and had a little money saved up in an old blue sock. She only withdrew from the sock for food and cooking gas. They could get by without electricity.

One day Providence delivered Señor Right straight to her front door. Felipe was a mild man, gentle and timid. His big serious eyes made her think of a stray puppy that had once been mistreated. He worked for the gas company and delivered the butane cylinders. Felipe was new on the route, very friendly and pleasant. He lightly flirted with her as he rolled a full cylinder off the truck, hooked up, and removed the empty. She often caught his eyes caressing her body when they were in conversation. Even though she was frugal and could make a cylinder last forever, Felipe came by on his run nearly every day and always stopped for coffee and while she filled his cup, he filled his eyes.

One day she was short of cash. "I don't have the full price of a cylinder today, Felipe," she said with embarrassment. By now they were on a first name second-person relationship. "I'll have to make it last till next week."

"What happens if your gas doesn't last until next week? Lucrecia, you can't eat raw beans."

"Oh, I'll be all right, really."

"Look, I can see you're already without electric power but you can't live without cooking gas. I'll install the new cylinder and you can pay me when you have the money." While he exchanged the cylinders he confessed he'd been looking for a place to stay.

Lucrecia, who was overwhelmed by his generosity, decided to be generous too. "You can stay here if you like. It's a little crowded but it won't cost you anything."

The arrangement was nothing less than perfect for all parties. The kids had an advocate to represent them in cases of misdemeanor. Lucrecia once again basked in the warm glow of kindness and the security that comes from knowing there's food in the house and gas in the cylinder. As for Felipe, he was king in his castle, installed on his Naugahyde throne, loved, respected, and graciously attended by his devoted court. Lucrecia made a comfortable home for him. He did all the little things around the house that needed doing but long neglected for lack of anyone to do them. They made plans to enlarge the house. The king settled with the power company and the lights were on again in the little brick house. Life was beautiful. Lucrecia's life was complete. Felipe couldn't get his fill of this young delicacy. He wanted her every night and Lucrecia was a generous girl.

But it turned out that there was a dead mouse in the salsa; Felipe had forgotten he already had a house in Tijuana with a wife, two teenage terrorists, and a guerilla invasion of his wife's relatives. The fuming señora made a surprise raid at his place of work. She took him firmly by the ear and led him away, to the amusement of his coworkers.

The lights in the little red brick house went out again. Felipe's progeny was now playing with a toy car.

Rrr-rrr-rrrr-rrrr.

The sound of the imaginary motor brought Lucrecia back to the present moment. Betito was gunning the engine now. His upper lip glistened from a viscous nasal discharge. It looked like olive oil.

Alone again. No husband, no *novio*, no man. No one. Lucrecia wanted nothing whatever to do with men again. Any man. She spoke to Concepcion in thought. "I suffered before I knew you and now I suffer for having known you. I could say I don't miss you but that would be a lie. I miss your smile, your arms, your mouth on my breast." Lucrecia didn't cry. There were no tears left in her to wash away the pain, and for lack of that rain that heals, the sediments of bitterness settled in her heart.

And now she'd found the way. Lucrecia in no way approved of the means to her ends. But she wasn't looking for approval, she was being practical. By now she'd learned not to depend on anyone, much less a man. She didn't need another charming *cabron* in her life. She alone would see that her children got by. Somehow. The security of her children was the only thing that got her up in the morning. Security by whatever means it took to achieve.

She heard a car.

"Go inside now, Betito, and tell Carmen to clean your nose."

Nyyrr-nyyrr-nyyrrr-nyyrrr. Betito threw the car into second and ran into the house.

Scenes from the past dissolved in the dusty heat as Lucrecia listened to the three girls bickering in the kitchen.

"I saw you holding hands with Lalo at school yesterday."

"So what! He's my *novio*. I'm almost fifteen, you know."

"Does he kiss you?"

"Are you going to tell?"

"Of course not. I promise."

"Yes, he kisses me. And I kiss him too."

"Do you let him touch you?"

"Of course! You do what boys want you to do. He's my *novio*."

"Is it nice? I mean, you know, when he touches you?"

"Of course, it's nice. It feels dreamy. I've got to start lunch now. Put the crayons away now and peel those two potatoes."

"In a minute."

"Now."

"You're so bossy!"

"I'm the oldest. I'm in charge when Mamá leaves on Saturdays."

"This potato is rotten."

"Cut out the bad part. It's about all we have."

"I can help too."

"Yes you can, Pilar. Wash that tomato. I'll fry it with some tortillas. That's lunch until Mamá gets home with provisions for the week."

"How do you know?"

"Because I know! Because when Mamá goes away in the car on Saturday she always come back with bags of groceries for the whole week — and sometimes even sweet cakes!"

"There's some peanut butter at the bottom of the jar."

"Good, scrape it all out and put it on a tortilla for Betito."

"He won't like it."

"He won't like it but he'll eat it."

"There's no milk in the house for Betito."

"I'll mix some cornmeal in water and load it with sugar. Betito will drink that."

Lucrecia was proud of Carmen. A resourceful girl for fourteen. She could always count on her to take charge of things. She stopped listening to her children in order to listen to a car still out of sight, her pretty face solemn as a requiem mass. In a minute the big car emerged from behind a thick fog of dirt. It was a new car, a shiny brown car. Lucrecia stood. Quickly, she put on her Saturday face and sauntered down the path like a high-fashion mannequin showing the latest Oscar de la Renta creation. The door opened. Her face burst into a smile that could make zinnias bloom in December, and she slipped inside.

The brown car drew away, sending a curling wave of brown powdery dust swirling toward the little brick house.

"I'll be fifteen next birthday. And when I'm fifteen I'm going to sit on the front steps. And you just watch. I'll come home with a new dress and all sorts of nice things."

"All for you, I suppose."

"No, for all of us. And sacks and sacks of food!"

"Now what are *you* crying about?"

"I want a car!"

"Carmen will bring you one, won't you?"

"Of course. And a truck too."

"And a fire engine?"

"And a fire engine."

"When?"

"When I'm fifteen."

"When will you be fifteen?"

"On my next birthday. And on Saturday I'll sit on the front steps in a pretty dress just like Mamá. And I'll ride in a big car. And when I get home we'll have everything!"

Hurricane Fermin

P *link!*
"I've lived in Tecate all my life and I don't remember ever seeing a storm as bad as this," the banker reminisced.

Hurricane Dora had been terrorizing the resort town of Mazatlan, ripping out palm groves, smashing fishing boats, and ravaging pristine beaches where Americans once gathered to recharge their solar cells. The tail end of the tropical storm flogged Tecate like a cat o' nine tails, bringing us raging winds and drenching rains. The plaza was under a foot of water and deserted. The only cars on the street were parked or abandoned. Chemo's taco cart lay across the hood of a police car awaiting the final sacrament. This was the second day without power and no telephone service.

Plink!

"It is also the worst storm I've ever seen," agreed the lawyer.

I was sitting with four of the hardiest Cafeteros, the coffee pot philosophers that convened every morning at La Fonda to discuss current events, solve domestic problems, make any number of peace proposals for the Middle East, and argue in heated voices over the best way to prepare *carne asada*. Our table was illuminated by two votive candles, the fireplace snapped and crackled pleasantly with a fragrant fire of eucalyptus logs. Our outer clothing hung on the backs of chairs. Soggy shoes and socks were lined up on the stone hearth as though waiting for Santa. We all looked like drowned cats and La Fonda smelled like a wet dog. Sergio the waiter placed an empty coffee can on our table to catch the occasional drip from the ceiling. While in the vicinity he refilled our cups.

Plink!

"Leave the coffee pot here, Sergio, and make another pot," the banker said. "We may be here for a few days." He took the sugar bowl, a Gerber's baby food jar with holes punched in the lid, and emptied half the contents into his cup of black coffee.

I found their quirky activity during the coffee ritual as fascinating as I did their conversation. "I had no idea hurricanes ever came up this far north," I commented.

"And this is only the tail," the ranchero with the waterlogged Pancho Villa mustache said, while he encouraged his two-story sombrero to resume its original shape.

"Señor *licenciado,* your jacket is smoking," Sergio advised the lawyer when he returned with a fresh coffee pot and a platter of dome-shaped sweet breads glistening with pink and white and yellow sugar. The *licenciado* moved his jacket away from the fire.

Plink!

Our poet/accountant stirred his coffee with a stick of cinnamon. "I remember the hurricane in '79. What a *desastre!* Every bridge between here and Ensenada was blown away by the floods."

"The worst disaster I can recall was in '82," the banker said. His meticulously trimmed mustache glistened with pink powdered sugar.

"There was no hurricane in '82." The *licenciado* was a stickler for accuracy.

Plink!

"No, I'm talking about the monetary crash when our wonderful government took over the banks and all our customers lost their dollar deposits." He looked mischievously at the coffee can catching the drips from the ceiling. It held only a few drops of water. With a sly wink at the others the banker quickly took the coffee can into the men's room. He returned with the can just short of overflowing and replaced it on the table.

Plonk!

"Well, what about Hurricane Fermin? Anybody here remember that?" The poet/accountant asked, licking his cinnamon stick.

"Who doesn't!" every Cafetero answered in a capella chorus.

"Objection! We're on the subject of *desastres naturales*," the lawyer insisted.

"But you have to admit Fermin Estrada was the worst natural disaster to ever hit Tecate!" the accountant laureate insisted.

"Sustained," the *licenciado* admitted.

"How come I never heard of him?" I asked. "And how did he come to earn the hurricane appellation?"

The ranchero placed a thick log on the fire. Sergio returned to our table and I thought he was good for at least a bronze in the standing high jump at the Pan American Games when he saw the coffee can overflowing onto the table. He ran to empty it and returned with a five-gallon bucket. "This is unbelievable. The roof always leaks but I've never seen it this bad!"

Plonk!

"It may have been before your time," the ranchero answered, having given up on restoring his sombrero. "And as to the sobriquet, the *cabron* Fermin was not from here. He was from Mexicali. And when he came to Tecate he came through like a hurricane!" The ranchero wrung moisture from his enormous mustache.

The doctor refilled my cup. "Let me begin the story. It happened about four years ago."

"Six." This from the lawyer.

The doctor acknowledged the amendment and continued. "At that time, that *cabron* Fermin Estrada was with Grupo Pirámide, S.A.de C.V., the largest insurance company in Mexico. When he was offered the Tecate office he jumped at it."

The *licenciado* poured milk into his coffee and suddenly remembered he was a lawyer. "Wait! Before we go on, let me make the following disclaimer." He took a big swallow of coffee then looked straight at me. "The opinions, actions, and behavior of the protagonist hereafter known as Fermin are his own and do not necessarily express the opinions of the reporters present here this morning, the Cafeteros as a group, their families or assigns. We are merely the chroniclers. No further warranty is expressed or implied."

Agreeing with the exceptions and conditions, the story of Fermin Estrada came to me from four sources, each filling in a detail forgotten or neglected by another. Now, I knew a lot of what they told me would be pure conjecture. They were intimate friends. They visited one another, they attended each other's weddings, baptismals, and funerals. But I don't think Fermin would have told them everything. And they couldn't possibly have been with him every hour of every day. But Tecate is a small pueblo. It is very much like a family. No one really has a secret. It took most of that wet and windy day, numerous pots of coffee, countless treks to the men's room, and later, a bottle of Tres Generaciones followed by a heavy lunch of *machaca*, *chiles rellenos*, enchiladas, rice, and beans. And now I pass this tale on to you. I'll begin in Mexicali where the beautiful Lydia Ramos, daughter of the renowned cardiologist, sat writing her wedding invitations.

Click, clack-clack.

Lydia ran her fingers over the roses embossed on the expensive white vellum. She felt a shiver of awe and curiosity, an aching pang of desire, still so full of mystery, course through her body. Inside the folded card in her hand was the authorization to lie naked beside Fermin Estrada on the night of June 26, 1997, and enter the intimate world of ecstasy as yet unknown. The honeymoon cabaña on the beach at Acapulco where they would celebrate the rites of marriage had been reserved weeks ago.

Click, clack-clack.

The bride-to-be sat at the long dining room table surrounded by three girlfriends who would soon serve as her bridesmaids and her maid of honor. Her grandmother, Mamá Juanita, sat on a rose-colored divan. The melodic clicking and clacking came from the wooden bobbins in her hands. She shifted the pegs over and under, around and back, in some magical order that would convert a spool of thread into the exquisite bobbin lace for the heirloom bridal veil she was meticulously restoring. These ladies were the only inhabitants of the house but for Perla, the servant girl. Both Lydia's parents had left earlier for an important gala in another part of Mexicali.

Lydia slipped the card into its matching envelope, addressed it from the list at her side, and passed it to Dorita who copied the names on the RSVP card and slipped it inside. Dorita then passed the assembled invitation to Carolina who adhered the postage and turned it over to Marta, the maid of honor designate, who sealed the envelopes and stacked them neatly in boxes.

Click, clack-clack.

"I'm glad we decided to do only a few each night. We only have fifty to go," Lydia said to the room.

"I can't believe we've addressed three hundred invitations," Dorita said.

"I can. My tongue has blisters!" Carolina answered.

Marta started to fill another box. "I'll take them all to the post office tomorrow."

"Everything seems to get more elaborate these days and less elegant." This from Mamá Juanita, whose comments and observations were not always relevant to the conversation in progress. "My mother was married in this veil and so was I. It is nearly a hundred years old. You just don't see things like this anymore."

The spicy fragrance of cinnamon and nutmeg reached the ladies as Perla entered the dining room almost without sound and placed a pitcher of hot chocolate and a plate of *empanadas* on the table. The little puff pastries, bursting with apricot preserve, were so light it appeared they would all float off the plate like helium balloons. Lydia left her place at the table and joined the queen dowager on the divan.

"Come, Mamá Juanita. Put that down and come have a *chocolatíto* with us."

"I will if you give me a moment." The wooden bobbins sounded like wind chimes as she carefully gathered them in one hand to prevent them from tangling. "Let me see something." She placed the work experimentally over Lydia's head. "The resemblance to your great-grandmother is remarkable. You have the same translucent complexion, the same raven hair. All the women of Andalusia are beautiful, you know. The only difference I see is that my mother's hair fell below her waist. And when I wore this veil my hair was so long and thick it was held with a huge silver comb. I still have the comb, but you don't have enough hair!"

The assembly line stopped, and all the ladies indulged in chocolate and *empanadas*. Mamá Juanita joined them at the table while continuing her line of thought. "Things are so different now. We hardly knew the man we married. We had to trust men blindly in those days."

"Things have changed, *abuelita*. I've known Fermin since we were children and I certainly can trust him with total confidence." Lydia passed a cup and a pastry to her grandmother.

Mamá Juanita only laughed. "You can see a man's face but you can't see his heart. Men are all the same on the inside, my dear. They haven't changed since the serpent spoke. All men pin the horns on their wives."

"Ay Mamacita!" Lydia exclaimed.

"Let me give you the same secret recipe for a successful marriage I gave your mother when she married your father."

Lydia prepared for something on the order of, manage the servants efficiently, cook only what he likes, don't contradict.

"Keep him broke, keep him on his toes — and above all — keep him limp!" The old woman's unexpected candor sent all the girls into fits of adolescent laughter. "And another thing — hire the homeliest servant girl you can find!"

"Your grandmother is absolutely right," Marta corroborated. "That's just the way men are."

"And you accept it?"

"Like mice in the pantry. I've been married almost three years now and I watch for signs every day."

"What on earth can you look for?" Lydia asked. "A brassiere in his pocket?"

Marta put down her cup and laughed. "Men aren't that careless but they are obvious. When a man starts to polish his car unnecessarily or suddenly starts using a fragrant after-shave, or spends more time in the bathroom than usual, it's a sure sign. And yes, I do check his pockets — I even smell his clothing!"

"Ay *Dios*! How awful! I couldn't do that." Lydia put another *empanada* on her plate. "The only defect that worries me about Fermin is his driving. He terrifies me! He drives like a *demónio*."

"Why don't you do the driving?" Dorita, who was now on her third *empanada*, suggested.

"I don't think that would help. I worry more when I'm not with him."

Carolina seemed uncomfortable with the topic. She bit into a pastry. "Is he coming by?"

"Yes, poor thing. He's driving all the way out from Tecate to be fitted for his tuxedo. He said he would get here around nine. I wonder if I should call the tailor shop and see if he's been there yet."

"*Dios mio*, you do worry so!"

"I just can't help it. Come, let's get the rest of these invitations done. I want to be through with all this when Fermin gets here."

Somewhere in Tecate Viviana looked over at the man she loved almost to the point of pain. Her lover tossed his head to get an incorrigible forelock of soft black hair out of his face and finished getting dressed. She loved that face too, the color of sandalwood, smooth as a boy's. Viviana didn't want it to end. Throwing back the sheet she leaped to his side naked without the tiniest twinge of self-consciousness. She put her arms around his waist and held him tight. She could feel the roughness of the embroidered design on the pocket of his shirt prickling her bare breast.

"Don't leave, *mi amor*. Do you really have to go now?"

Fermin looked at his watch. *Madre!* It was after eight and Lydia was expecting him at nine. And he still had to stop for a fitting. I'll have to average four hundred miles an hour, he thought.

"*Sí, mi amor.* I have to attend the rosary for my friend Balderas and it's on the other side of town."

"Promise me I'll see you soon."

"I promise."

"Kiss me again before you go."

Fermin bent his head to hers, but she took a step back and held out her breasts to him. "Here."

Viviana didn't realize it at that tender moment but she had just been summarily kissed off. Fermin ran out the door. As far as he was concerned it was time to say adios. Viviana could be a lot of fun but she was starting to get clingy. Women are all the same, he grumbled. As soon as you make love to them it's *promise me I'll see you soon*!

Once behind the wheel of his cadmium orange Camaro, he catapulted out of the parking lot, down Tecate's only main avenue, and got on the treacherous highway to Mexicali. With God's help he made it to Mexicali alive. He had about another five miles to go but traffic was thick. He squeaked through several yellow traffic lights, streaked through a couple of red ones with impunity, and screeched to a stop in front of a building that looked like it would be condemned by the end of the week. The place looked closed. He would be in deep caca if it was. A dim light glowed inside. Thank God they're still open! He pushed through the door. It was unbearably stuffy but the pretty young girl behind the desk provided instant resuscitation.

"*Buenas tardes.*" The voice was smooth, round, and fluty. The girl, with short fluffy hair, and still in her tender teens, wore a yellow sweater that she appeared to be outgrowing as she spoke.

It took Fermin a few seconds to gain speech. "Forgive me for staring, señorita. *Buenas tardes.* I am a student of architecture and I have never seen such an exquisite example of classical moldings, planes, and curves."

The classical structure behind the desk smiled her appreciation and blushed to the follicles. "You are Nuñez?"

"For you I would be Nuñez, Lopez, Garcia," he gripped his heart with both hands. "Calderon...Martinez...Benito Juarez, if you like, Vicente Fox! But I have no option but to confess that I am Estrada, your humble *servidor.*" He went down on one knee and began searching the floor with his hands.

"What are you looking for?"

"My heart!"

Just as this friendship was beginning to burst from bud to full flower, a Rottweiler in a white shirt and baggy dark trousers appeared from behind a screen. Fermin figured he had snapped his leash then realized it was a tape measure around his neck. "*Sí* señor, you are with the Nuñez family?"

"No Papá, he is Vicen— Estrada!"

Fermin came to his feet and now it was his turn to blush. "I phoned earlier about a tuxedo fitting."

The pretty young thing's father quickly recognized the fox in his yard, down on one knee leering at his daughter and tossing *piropos* like confetti. "You can lock the door now, Sonya, and go to the house." Obediently, his daughter locked the front door and disappeared behind the screen that doubtless led to the family's living quarters. Then the little man with the Rottweiler grin turned to Fermin. "Step this way, señor."

Fermin wasn't sure he wanted to but he did.

Even the casual reader will quickly see that Lydia was hardly finished addressing her wedding invitations when the *sopa* was already beginning to thicken.

In time, Lydia's invitations were delivered, her dresses made, and the Church of Our Lady de Guadalupe filled to capacity with family and friends and the curious. Father Cosme said the nuptial Mass. Like all brides, Lydia was beautiful. When the bride and groom reached the front steps for pictures, they were legally married. In any event, they had been married in a civil ceremony in the presence of a judge day before yesterday. This was done because neither the State nor the Church accepts the other's marriage as valid currency.

As in the case of all weddings, it was at the reception where my narrators picked up much of the interesting information. A little nosegay of Lydia's old school friends in frothy dresses gathered around the punch bowl.

"Where did Lydia ever unearth a man like that? He's beautiful! Do you know anything about him?"

"I do not know the Estradas, but it is my understanding that his father is a *Persona Importante* somewhere."

A gentleman with enough snow in his hair to authenticate his observation made comment in the company of a cynical chuckle. "My dear ladies, in Mexico *Personas Importantes* are as common as dandelions. Everyone is connected to a *Persona Importante*. The power worshippers in our society demand it!"

At the buffet table another group of the bride's best friends gathered to snitch and tell while attacking a vast selection of expensive canapés.

"The most desirable bachelor in the region has been escorted out of the arena." This was hissed by an attractive brunette wrapped in peach chiffon. She took two canapés, one with sausage, the other with shrimp, turned on her matching pumps, and swirled away from the group.

"I think she's hurt."

"I think she's simmering with jealousy," one of the girls from Tecate said. "Viviana was in his bed for nearly a year. She had her chance and lost."

"Unfortunately what she lost cannot be regained."

"From what I've heard, being married to Fermin is going to be like keeping a Hereford bull in the yard without a nose ring."

"I think you're misplacing the location of the ring."

"For the life of me, what does Fermin see in that little mouse?"

"Mouse! With her hair so short and that long neck she looks more like a goose in white taffeta."

Not far from the bride's best friends, a group of Fermin's intimates, including a few of the Cafeteros, were also making their observations.

"Well, how long do you think it will last?"

"Until the wee hours of the morning, at least."

"No, no, I mean the *matrimonio*."

"I give it six months or the birth of the baby, whichever comes first."

"I assure you Lydia walked to the altar a virgin. Don't ask me how I know."

"How did she manage that? I thought Fermin exhausted the supply of immaculate señoritas. Remember what happened to Clarita at the bank?"

"And Conchita at the telephone company."

"And don't forget Susi!"

"Do you think this will tame the fox?"

Predictably, the wedding fiesta lasted until dawn. The bride and the groom, who over-indulged in drink, spent what remained of the night in separate rooms in the home of his parents. On Sunday morning, a friend of the groom's whisked them to Tijuana International Airport to catch the Aeromexico flight to Acapulco.

Ten days later Aeromexico Flight No. 119 from Acapulco taxied to the gate and a hundred and fifty sun-bronzed passengers with festive faces entered the Tijuana terminal to return to the real world of job and duty. The glitz of the disco, the cha-cha-cha, near-naked bodies glistening in the emerald sea, and sipping piña coladas under a *palapa* while mariachis played, would be little more than a memory tomorrow.

Fermin and Lydia followed the crowd to the taxi stand and headed home. That year summer had swept into Tecate with flame and torch. It was July. The buildings surrounding the plaza quivered in the intense heat. The dirt roads were cracked and they looked like peanut brittle. All the trees and shrubs writhed in agony and cried for water. There was only dust, fine as cake flour, where there should have been air. Every living soul was indoors, barricaded behind curtains and shutters. The dogs and cats called a truce and shared the oily shade under parked cars and the soothing darkness under wooden stoops, sanctuary of the rodents and black widows. Even the summer flies defected, and went into hiding. The town was suffocating under the heavy weight of an airless day seething under a white sun that intensified the blue sky with no beginning and no end.

The bedroom of the small apartment still held the heat of the day. The late afternoon sun beat on the glass pane, backlighting the red and yellow poppies on the curtains so the window resembled a bright Chinese paper lantern.

The insatiable lovers lay on pale lavender sheets still crisp and fresh-smelling from the clothesline. Her slender body was tanned from the sun, her smooth skin the color of cinnamon. The only thing covering her was the faint glow of her desire. Her eyes were closed but they were dark as agate. The man who made all her dreams come true lay nestled in her slender arms. She admired the bronze plating on his muscular body that ended in a sharp line of white skin above his smooth, round *nalgas*.

"I love you," she murmured softly.

"And I love you."

"I have been aching for you."

"Sometimes I love you so much it hurts."

The two lovers were oblivious of anything beyond their touch. While they searched and surrendered to each other, little white wisps came floating across the sky over Tecate. Gradually they grew into curly cock's feathers, ragged and snowy white. And with all the speed of things unobserved, the wind, like giant bellows, gathered the clouds against the low hills of Cuchuma until they were stacked on top of each other and they became towering palisades of gray granite. The clouds turned dark and angry. In a matter of minutes their puffy white tops flattened and now they looked like enormous black anvils. Neither lover noticed the room suddenly darken and the Chinese lantern go out.

"You have me on fire!"

"Kiss me again like that."

"Yes!"

Jagged slashes of blinding orange lightning leaped across the boulders in the sky. From somewhere beyond the frontiers of reality came the warning, a low trembling rumble. The lovers were unaware. Their mission was now so urgent the Earth could have fallen out of the galaxy and they wouldn't have known. Or cared. Sheaves of driving rain, orphans of a hurricane four hundred miles to the south, coursed down the window like tears. Neither heard.

"*Mi amor!*"

"Yes?"

"Do that again."

"That?"

"Yes, I love it!"

A flash of lightning. A sudden explosion of thunder ripped the sky and rattled the house like an earthquake. The lovers were only momentarily startled. They were beyond return to the world outside. The sky poured out its contents with a deafening roar that made no sound for them. The pool of their desire began to fill.

She opened her eyes briefly, seeking confirmation in his face. She closed them again and let herself float away to wait for him in that sweet darkness on the other side of reason. Her mouth was soft, her lips parted slightly, a little whimper escaping. Tiny droplets formed like dew on her upper lip.

"Now, *mi amor,* now!"

"*Sí, mi amor, sí!*"

"Don't stop, *mi amor.* Don't stop! Don't stop!"

The deep pool of their passion was full beyond containment. It could no longer hold back the forces within it. There was a sudden explosion as the gates burst and they were consumed by a flood of ecstasy that overflowed the banks of their souls.

All was peace, all was quiet. He lay beside her nuzzling in the softness of her shoulder. He could hear the rain now sluicing down the windowpane. He could hear himself breathing. Minutes went by before he propped himself on one elbow in order to shower little kisses on her face. He always kissed her afterward. Tears rained down her cheeks.

"Why do you cry, my darling?"

She turned over and buried her face deep into the sheet. "Because I love you."

"That's a silly reason to cry." He slapped her *nalgas* playfully.

"I'm going to lose you."

"Lose me! How can you say that? We just got back from our honeymoon yesterday."

"Yes, but you're married now. Don't you understand, Fermin? You won't have time for me..." and she gave herself up to tears.

Fermin softened his voice. "Estela, my darling."

"What?"

"Have I ever failed you?"

"No, but —"

"No, but what?"

"But it's different now."

"Different!"

"Things won't be the same."

"Fa! Nothing is going to change. How can you say that? We just got off the plane yesterday. I still have sand in my hair, and I'm here, no?"

She came out of his arms and sat up in bed, pulling the top sheet up to her chin to hide her breasts that had been his only minutes ago.

Fermin threw his bronzed legs over the side and began to get dressed. "Nothing is going to change. Lydia knows I'm no saint."

"She know about me?"

"Not about you." Not about the others either, he told himself. "We never talk about it." He was fully dressed now. "And let me add that Lydia and I don't do the same things you and I do."

Estela experienced a surge of superiority. She hooked the top sheet with her toes and pulled it down again. "Do you have to go now?"

"Yes, I must, she expects me home every day at six."

The sky cleared. Neither noticed the Chinese lantern come on again. The matinee closed and the wind took its entire company of players racing toward the east and the Sierra Rumorosa for the evening performance. Fermin walked to the door. "It looks like we had some rain. See you tomorrow." And Fermin Estrada walked into the wet street and headed for his new home and his new bride to tell the first of a million lies.

Lydia was in her new home, a neo-colonial structure with a charming front courtyard and a singing fountain of pink stone located in one of the new *colonias*. She was putting away wedding gifts. There was glassware to be washed and put away, along with linens and silver pieces. The servant girl came but once a week and following her grandmother's advice, she'd hired the homeliest wench she could find. She'd only been a wife for a few weeks but already was enjoying the role of Señora Lydia Estrada. They both had a large circle of friends and it was fun to go out to dinner or dancing then come home and get into bed as man and wife. One day she would learn to do the things he liked. Even when alone she blushed at the thought. She really didn't know what to expect, certainly her mother never talked about it, neither did her girlfriends, married or single. She found the whole thing mysterious, tender, delicious, and exquisite.

Lydia moved to the bedroom and began to put away the trail of clothing Fermin was in the habit of leaving behind him; a blue sock on the floor, its mate rolled up inside his underwear. She slipped the navy blue blazer that lay crumpled on a chair onto a hanger, placed it in the closet, and froze. His pockets? Lydia, you are terrible! Married only a few weeks and already suspicious. I'm not suspicious! It's just that I know him. When he takes it to the cleaners he'll forget to empty the pockets and he'll lose something important. Once she found justification, the search warrant was signed and served. She found nothing in the inside breast pocket. The right pocket, empty. From the left pocket she withdrew a cocktail napkin from El Sombrero in Tijuana. A phone number was scribbled under the red and green sombrero. Lydia, she scolded, you're being silly. Probably a client. With a pang of guilt she put it out of her mind.

Fermin sat in his corner office on the top floor of the Guajardo Building, Tecate's only high-rise. This put him on the second floor. He had three expensively furnished offices and two well-equipped secretaries. He was on intimate terms with both, in a physical sense, that is. But they finally tired of waiting for an invitation to join him at the altar, or at the very least, share his apartment. And so they both took husbands who were not aware that they weren't getting new merchandise. It was a good arrangement, of course, as mutual culpability made it highly unlikely that indiscreet comments would reach Lydia.

Fermin held the phone away from his ear. He was listening to the sonic booms of his boss melting the telephone cable that stretched from Tijuana to his desk.

"Welcome back from your honeymoon, Fermin," he shouted.

"*Gracias.*"

"Your numbers look terrible this month," the man shouted.

Fermin pulled the phone away from his ear. He heard the same recital every month even when his numbers were good. "We'll end the month with some good figures."

"Good. By the way, why haven't you reported back to the doctor for the second half of your health evaluation?"

"I just got back to the office this week." He could hear traffic noise and a siren in the background.

"This town is driving me crazy. Every time I get on the phone somebody calls for an ambulance!" There was a pause while the siren faded away. "Well, get over there tomorrow. We have a huge investment in all our executives. We want to make sure they stay healthy. Tomorrow, *sí*? I will call Dr. Bolaños and tell him you'll be there."

The next morning Fermin raced his Camaro to Tijuana for the purpose of finishing his physical examination and maybe doing a complete physical on the little chile pepper who played hostess at El Sombrero where he thought he might as well have lunch. By eleven o'clock he sat waiting impatiently in Dr. Bolaños's examining room.

Presently, a little sparrow of a man, skinny as a dinner fork in a floor-length white lab coat, walked in. His face consisted mostly of nose blooming under thick tortoiseshell glasses and a shamelessly naked pate rimmed with light frost. He had that glowing rosy-pink complexion common to those individuals who have consecrated their life to health. He greeted his patient cordially. "*Buenos días*, Fermin!" Fermin answered with the same words but he didn't believe it. "You're in good health, Fermin, I can't find anything wrong with you." He sounded almost disappointed. "Blood pressure is normal, lungs are clean. You're in good shape. The only thing I don't like is this." He brought out a laboratory report from Fermin's folder. "Your cholesterol is too high... Too high." He wrinkled his rosy brow. "You have a cholesterol count of 200! Unacceptable." Dr. Bolaños seemed to be near a seizure himself.

"Are those high numbers?"

"High?— they're in the stratosphere!"

"Cut out red meat, milk, butter, eggs of course, ice cream, cheese, and other animal fats. More fruits and vegetables. I want to see that number down to at least 140. Come and see me in six months with some good numbers." He patted Fermin firmly on the shoulder. Fermin could feel every bone in his hand through his shirt. "It's the same diet I follow myself and look at me at seventy-four years of age!" Fermin was not impressed. What's the point of being healthy if you don't have any fun?

The numbers had absolutely no meaning for Fermin. How could he control it? He couldn't see the numbers go up or down every time he had a plate of *carne asada* with a side of guacamole or a cheese enchilada. Sure, he grumbled to himself, I'll switch to tofu tacos and alfalfa sprout burritos. I'll drink my coffee black and eat *chiles rellenos* stuffed with yogurt. I'll eat birdseed for dessert in place of flan with caramel sauce. But Fermin had no option but to agree to another visit.

He went directly from the doctor's office to El Sombrero. The gorgeous little creature wasn't there and he was seated by a willowy individual of undetermined sex. He was about to order his favorite medley of saturated fats when Dr. Bolaños slipped into the booth.

"What a pleasant surprise!" the doctor said.

"Yes."

"We can enjoy a healthful lunch together. How are things in Tecate?"

Fermin was forced to order, and eat, a salad that would have sent a rabbit into raptures. By the time he got home it was close to nine o'clock and he was not in high spirits. Lydia did not fail to make the observation.

This was probably not the propitious time to put her grandmother's advice into practice. But Lydia had no experience of her own to draw from, and metaphorically speaking, the Inquisition began.

"Where have you been? I was worried sick. The way you drive terrifies me! I expected you home hours ago. Who were you with so late?" She saw her husband teeter slightly in an attempt to regain his balance. Now she understood what Mamá Juanita meant. Keep him broke, keep him on his toes — and keep him limp!

"I was in Tijuana on important business most of the day and it has not been a wonderful day. Is this the greeting I get?"

His plea filled Lydia with remorse. "You poor thing, sit down and let me take care of you," her voice was gentle as a cradle song. She removed his shoes and rubbed his feet. "There, that better?"

Now, Fermin thought, this is the kind of wife a man is entitled to by decree. "Something smells awfully good."

"Pork chops in *chile verde*, refried beans, flour tortillas that will melt in your mouth and a very rich flan that I made this afternoon."

"With caramel sauce?"

"With caramel sauce."

Fermin ate voraciously, as the little twigs and sticks with Dr. Bolaños was all he'd taken all day. Lydia will make a good wife, he thought. She just needs someone strong to channel her in the right direction. It is probably a good thing that modern science has yet to come up with a means of tapping into the mind because his fantasies wandered off in the direction of Tijuana. Maybe he could go back to El Sombrero later this week. He managed to get the hostess' name. Susi. I'll take her to a nice disco. Cha-cha-cha, merengue, bamba. I wonder how mellow she gets after a few margaritas? No! I'll invite her to the beach — at night — yes! Swimming nude in the moonlight! What an extraordinary device, the human mind, he thought. I'm swimming naked with Susi while I have dinner with my wife! "You are a wonderful little wife, *mi amor*," he said as Lydia brought him a second helping of beans and a few more tortillas.

But of course, Lydia also possessed a mind equally insulated against eavesdroppers. She gave him her sweetest smile. "Oh, by the way, I'll need an extra four hundred U.S. dollars this week, *mi amor*."

"Four hundred dollars! Are you buying a car?"

Lydia ruffled his hair playfully. "No, silly, but we do need a few things and I don't have any summer clothes."

They'd only been married a few weeks. Where were all her clothes? Did all women enter into marriage stark naked! But Fermin not only had a dark past, he also had a much darker present that had to be concealed at all costs. "*Sí*, of course, *mi amor*, I'll leave you a check tomorrow before I leave." He would have to scramble for play money this week.

Lydia was pleased with her first reading of Mamá Juanita's script. He smells suspicion on my breath, she told herself. That's good. I don't know whether he's putting the horns on me or not, but I'm going to continue to accuse him just for the doubts. He will at least have to be careful. And now the money he would have squandered out on the street is safe with me. Mamá Juanita is a wellspring of wisdom, she thought. The only item remaining is to keep him limp and that will not be hard.

The months fell off the calendar like leaves in October and Fermin and Lydia fell into a familiar pattern. She nagged, she scolded. She developed her carping into something of an art form. Fermin, on the other hand, claimed innocence but chafed at the tight rein. Secretly he justified his actions as a birthright under Natural Laws which mandate a man's right to do as he pleases.

It didn't take Fermin long to discover Marisol, a sweet new flower in the garden of the Department of Tourism. When she asked about his wife, Fermin explained to her that his marriage had been in a state of decay for some time. He implied that separation was imminent and promised marriage just as soon as the lawyers had it all sorted out. And Marisol eagerly drained the cup of sweet deceit. He also threw in a line about a love that would burn until the universe itself expired. When Marisol began to show Fermin was in a state of uncontrollable panic. But once again he was saved by the ironies of Fate. Her parents packed her off to her grandparents in Guadalajara "to continue her studies at the university." God, that was a close call! He gasped. Why can't women take more precautions? At least she's across the country and out of my life.

A few weeks later Fermin burned up the road to El Sombrero in Tijuana and finally succeeded in making his move on Susi. On her evening off he took her to the seashore at Playas de Tijuana, equipped with a blanket, a basket of cheeses, crackers, pickled mushrooms, and a chilled bottle of Cordon Negro. They nibbled at the treats, while he refilled their glasses with the bubbly. He did not make a move. The outing was as wholesome as a Sunday school picnic. He talked about marriage and commitment and a love that would endure until man uttered his last syllable on earth. This was one of Fermin's favorite vignettes. It never failed to achieve the desired results.

"Oh Fermin, you say such beautiful and profound things. I don't know what to say."

"Say you love me."

"I love you."

"Say that we will consecrate our love with our bodies and our souls and two hearts will become one."

"*Sí, mi amor, sí!* But where can we go?"

"How would you like it if we delivered our love to one another under a silver moon on a deserted beach?" Susi may have been imagining a beach in Puerto Vallarta. She answered him with a long kiss. Fermin was thinking more along the lines of Ensenada.

The following week Fermin took Susi to a deserted beach, a venue he knew well just south of the little seaside town. The night was profoundly dark, as the moon had not yet made its appearance. They stood beside his car in a tight embrace inhaling the erotic sea air. The crashing of the waves, the hiss of the foam lapping on the sand, provided the music and effects track. Their kisses were long and demanding. By the time he had removed some of her wardrobe in order to gain access to warm skin, the moon complied with orbital orders and the sea was covered with shards of silver.

His next move was crucial. The phrasing, the mannerism, the gestures had to be no less than perfect. "Do you love me?" This was whispered through her long hair into her left ear.

"Oh, Fermin, I love you like I've never loved before or ever will again."

So far so good. "Come."

She followed him to the back of the car." I have all the picnic things in the trunk. We will spread our blanket down by the water and give ourselves without reserve." He watched the expression on her face.

"O, *sí, mi amor, sí!*"

So far so good, he mused. Now here comes the hard part. Fermin left her for a moment, locked the car, returned to her, and opened the trunk. He removed his shirt and tossed it carelessly into the trunk.

"What are you doing?"

"We will go down to meet the sea in a natural state." He saw her hesitate. He quickly crossed his arms in front of him, peeled off his T-shirt and threw it in recklessly.

Susi slowly, timidly removed her blouse. "Can anyone see us?"

Fermin perceived she was starting to get nervous. He'd been through the drill a hundred times. "Impossible!" He tossed his shoes and socks. The only thing in sight was the feeble glow of yellow light coming from La Tortuga, a rowdy cantina half a mile up the beach.

Susi placed her blouse in the trunk. Her bra had already been unclasped and came away with the blouse. Fermin knew from long experience on this very beach that the next move was a very delicate matter. He interrupted the disrobing ceremonies and put his arms around her tightly but gently.

"This moment is ours forever. Tonight we make memories." He released her as gently as he had taken her in his arms. In one swift move he was out of his slacks and underwear and stood before her *puris naturalibus*. He held his arms open wide like the angels do when they're offering a blessing.

With an urgency that surprised Susi and pleased Fermin, her jeans and slinky briefs joined his clothes in the trunk. Fermin took the angel pose again and Susi took shelter in his open arms. They held each other quietly for an endless moment, feeling the heat from their naked bodies cast in silver, listening to the music of the sea. It was time to walk her down to the water's edge for an unforgettable night of ecstasy.

"Come my love." He held her gently with his right hand, quietly closed the trunk lid with his left, and began to escort her toward the sand dunes.

"Don't we need the blanket?"

"Of course, of course. It's in the — *Madre de Dios... Virgencita de la Caridad*!!" This double appeal to divine deities for immediate succor was gasped with double exclamation points.

"What is it?"

The voice was tiny, as though spoken through a soda straw. "I just locked everything in the trunk."

"Dear God!"

"Don't panic."

"I'm not panicked." She dropped his hand like she would drop a dead frog. "Do you have anything in the car to cover us?"

"No, and we can't get in anyway. I locked it first."

It took Susi less than a second to fully metabolize this distressing piece of information. "We can't stand out here naked all night," she hissed like a cat with its tail pressed under somebody's foot. How would she ever get home? She had a disturbing vision of her father opening the front door for her.

"Follow me."

"Where are we going?" There was a noticeable change of tone in her voice. It was no longer husky and mellow with passion. It was streaked with anger.

"We will be safer behind the sand dunes. Maybe then I can figure out how to get a locksmith down here."

"Why, that's a wonderful idea. And he can work on the lock while we stand around STARK NAKED AND WATCH!" She spat the words in his face.

"I'll think of something."

They took shelter behind the dunes and sat in what can best be described as a prickly silence. The soft silvery moonlight now illuminated them like stadium lights. The romantic music of the surf became a nerve-racking noise. A short, icy interval passed, then both heard it at the same time. Footsteps! Someone crunching along the sand. Someone headed directly toward where they stood! Immediately they came to their feet, adrenaline pumping, prepared for flight. They were too late. A grungy derelict dressed in rags, roaring drunk, and reeking of everything foul, stepped directly in front of them.

"God save me! Adam and Eve!" The mendicant made the cross in the air. "I have entered into Paradise."

It was a moment of pure inspiration for Fermin and he lost no time. He tackled the drunkard like a defensive linebacker. There was a musical chinking sound as his plastic bag of aluminum cans hit the sand and the man was deep in a tequila coma.

"What are you doing?" Susi screamed in a hoarse whisper.

"I'm going to get us out of here."

No one will ever know with certainty whether it was the fright of the physical attack, or the shock experienced at the sudden apparition of Adam and Eve, but the bum never stirred. He lay in a sound sleep under a silver moon in the company of the murmuring music of the sea.

In a matter of seconds Fermin had the old man's clothes off. He tossed the shirt over to Susi. "Here put this on." He was in the man's pants by the time he finished the sentence.

"Are you serious? It's filthy!"

"Don't complain, I'm wearing pants soaked in piss and vomit. Stay here naked if you like. I'm going to get a locksmith."

Susi immediately saw the logic in Fermin's suggestion. She slipped into the offensive garment and was relieved to see the shirttails reached her knees. She followed Fermin.

"Where are we going?"

"To that cantina a half mile up. It will be faster."

She followed in silence as no one was in a chirpy mood. In a few minutes they gained La Tortuga and Fermin gave her instructions. "Stay out here in the dark. I'm just going to stick my head in the door."

With no other option open to her, Susi did as instructed. Fermin pushed open the swinging doors, took one step inside and froze in place. The gloomy waterfront bar was about as dark inside as it was outside and smelled as bad as his borrowed pants. Through a thick fog of illegal smoke he saw the toughest men he'd ever seen. Some gathered around scarred tables, others leaned on the bar. All looked dangerously drunk. He wondered how many were armed. The fierce-looking bartender did not look too cordial either. Fermin noticed the dark man had only one eye and a vicious scar extending from the corner of his mouth to his ear. He glared at Fermin who was too terrified to walk in any farther.

He stood there naked to the waist, fighting to keep his voice from soaring like the coloratura soprano in Carmen when she's stabbed by Don José and revealing the fear he felt in his gut. "I need a locksmith," he squeaked.

The bartender rolled his only eye. "They're all locksmiths here," he said with a sweep of the hand to indicate all the occupants of the den.

"I've got twenty U.S.dollars for the first man who can get into my car."

"Anyone of these *cabrones* can do that for you in less time than it takes them to take a leak. You don't have to pay them!" A clatter of dirty laughter came though the haze.

There was a mad scramble as vagrants, competent car thieves, and very probably murderers, raced for the door.

"I'll take you," Fermin said, pointing to a swarthy man with seaweed hair who looked dangerous but appeared to be more sober than the others. "Come with me."

The two walked silently back along the dark deserted beach. Susi followed behind them. They found the car. In less time than it took to write this paragraph the trunk lid flew open. Fermin reached for his pants, dug out a twenty, and shoved it in the man's hand. The old man of the sea, listing slightly for lack of ballast, set sail for La Tortuga on an unsteady port tack and disappeared.

Fermin and Susi discarded their filthy rags and got into their clothes. They drove home in icy silence. Fermin covered the seventy-five miles of twists and turns in less than an hour. Susi crossed herself a hundred times.

He pulled up in front of her parent's house and spoke for the first time. "I want you to know I think the world of you." He was definitely trying to salvage something from the wreckage.

"I would be even more flattered if you had no opinion of me at all."

"Well, at least we made some memories."

"I sincerely hope that we have not. This very night I will call on the Blessed Virgin to erase this day from my mind forever."

"Aren't you going to kiss me good night?"

Susi stepped out of the car. "I'm going to pretend I never met you."

"Unreasonable *sangrona*!" Fermin grumbled, screeching away from the curb. He had no emotional investment in Susi, or any other of his playthings, but still it rankled him to let a good-looking *chamaca* like Susi slip through the cracks.

But the worst of the evening was yet to come. Lydia could smell him before he walked in the door. His arraignment began at once. There were angry words and denials, tricky questions designed to trip up the suspect that he couldn't answer. It was more than Fermin could handle in one day. He was obliged to sleep on the couch. He mumbled a feeble prayer to anybody who might be listening — may tomorrow be a better day.

Even in Tecate where punctuality is unknown the iambic march of Time moves inexorably onward. The Christmas holidays were here along with Fermin's six-month appointment with Dr. Bolaños.

"I am very disappointed, Fermin. Disappointed," Dr. Bolaños announced as he walked into the examining room shaking his head to the rhythm of the syllables. You are not only heavier than you were six months ago, your cholesterol is…" He withdrew the laboratory report from his file and tapped it ominously with the back of his fingers. "…worse than before. 220! And you are eight kilos overweight. Unacceptable, Fermin, unacceptable. You're going to have a heart attack and die before you're thirty-five!"

The pink little man with the big nose in the white coat made Fermin feel like a schoolboy in front of the headmaster. He didn't want to listen to this. "It's married life, doctor. I try, I really do. Yesterday I only had two apples for lunch. This morning breakfast was black coffee and small piece of fruit," he said with a mouthful of lies. "I told my wife to fix me a spinach salad with nothing over it but lemon juice for dinner." He lubricated every word with sincerity.

"And what are you doing about lunch today?"

"I have a bag of carrots in the car."

Dr. Bolaños wasn't fooled. He handed his patient a printed sheet. "Here is the diet I want you to follow and an exercise program. I want to see you here again in six months if you're still alive. *Feliz Navidad.*"

Fermin left the office agitated. So much authority, it was worse than being a child. Authority from his wife, authority from his boss, and then these ridiculous and impossible demands from that little bald-headed doctor. When he got to his car he tossed the instruction sheets on the floor and headed for Burritos Shalom, his favorite place for *carnitas*. He needed sustenance. After emptying a plastic basket of succulent pork, tortillas, guacamole, and two Coronas, he felt whole again. It was now time for some form of relaxation. He flipped through his mental Rolodex. As long as he was in Tijuana he might as well look up a little diversion. El Sombrero was off limits. He didn't want to face Susi and he could run into Dr. Bolaños eating his cottage cheese and fruit. Better pass on Tijuana. On the way home at 90 mph on the toll road, Fermin thought of Irma Bustamante. Passionate dark eyes, lots of soft brown hair, big mangos, and always willing. Her image warmed his heart. Irma worked in City Accounting. She got off at three. She would be home by the time he got there and would provide a bit of tinsel on the Christmas season that hadn't yet begun to sparkle with joy and good tidings. Just what Dr. Bolaños ordered; low in saturated fats, no cholesterol, and good cardiovascular exercise.

The following week Fermin and Lydia were on their way to her parents' home for the Christmas *posadas*. There is only the treacherous Rumorosa Mountain pass connecting Tecate to Mexicali just as there is only one Khyber Pass from Pakistan to Afghanistan. Both share the same characteristics; narrow, unmarked lanes and hairpin turns, perilous switchbacks, and unguarded cliffs offering a thousand foot free-fall to the careless. Tonight the corrugated road was covered with snow and visibility was limited to the flurries reflected in the headlights. Fermin negotiated the turns on two wheels, the Camaro fishtailing around every bend. Paralyzed with fear, Lydia prayed and drew the cross the whole way over just as she knew she would all the way home. This man will one day kill us both, she thought.

When all the Christmas parties were over on Twelfth Night, life resumed its normal course for the Estradas. They sat at the breakfast table, Lydia still in her satin blue robe and matching slippers, drinking coffee.

Fermin was already dressed for the office and stared resentfully at the plate of fruit in front of him. "I may be a little on the late side getting back from Tijuana tonight."

"Oh, another *meeting?*"

Fermin perceived the italics in her voice. He took a sip of coffee. "Yes, another *meeting.*" He gave the word back to her freighted with dignity and importance. "And we don't start until four or five o'clock." Then he referred to the offensive breakfast before him. "How am I expected to survive on this? I need eggs and sausage."

Lydia regretted her earlier sarcasm and stirred artificial sweetener into her words. "Eat it, *mi amor,* it's for your own good. Dr. Bolaños is right. I don't want you to get sick. I love you."

"I love you too, *corazón.*" When Fermin told his wife that he loved her he wasn't lying intentionally. Under the heavy chains of his machismo Fermin really did love his wife to the extent that he was capable. You might love a particular piece of music but you're not going to listen to the same song night after night after night for the rest of your life, he told himself. I meet my obligations by providing everything my wife wants. Beyond that, what I do is nobody's business. I don't have to justify myself to anyone! He told her what he wished could be true. "You're right, *mi amor.* This new year I start a new life. No more eating everything in sight, no more late nights drinking with the *amigos.*" *Amigas* would have been closer to the truth. He ate some fruit to lend his words validity, kissed his wife, and went out the door. He would stop at the Taco Contento on his way to work for a decent breakfast.

Lydia heard him peel rubber as he pulled away. She ran immediately to her dresser and found the folded paper Mamá Juanita slipped to her in secret during the holiday fiestas. How that sweet old woman ever came to know a sorceress in Tecate she couldn't even begin to imagine. Lydia asked no questions when her grandmother gave her the paper and was offered no explanations.

It was mid-morning when Lydia pulled into a dirt track at the foot of the sacred mountain of Cuchuma and followed it cautiously until she came to a rustic gate. A bedspring really, between two wooden posts with a rope across the opening. She parked and approached. Quiet. Not a soul around. The yard behind the bedspring was a veritable jungle of pungent weeds and herbs. Then she saw the little bell tied to the bedspring with a piece of bailing wire. She shook the bell, filling the warm spicy air with silvery tinkles. She could perceive movement somewhere in the jungle.

In a few seconds a diminutive Oaxaca Indian figure materialized and Lydia was looking into a copper-plated face with a smile as bright as the sun. Her blouse was white with white embroidery. Swirls of purple, from the darkest maroon to the palest lilac, covered the long skirt. She tinkled with bracelets on both arms. A ring flashed from every finger and long gold earrings grazed her shoulders. Aromatic smoke curled up from a length of rope she held in her hand. Lydia was starting to have second thoughts about coming here and if there had been a dignified way of bolting for home, she would have done it.

"*Buenos dias.*" The voice was rich and bigger than its tiny container.

"*Buenos dias,*" Lydia returned uncertainly. "Are you — are you Doña Tichi?"

"Yes, and you are Lydia, no?"

She almost said, how did you know? But Lydia was stunned and for a moment without speech. She had never seen this strange little witch in her life! When her voice returned she said, "Do you know me?"

"Aren't you the granddaughter of Doña Juanita?"

"Yes, but how did you know?" She couldn't hide the incredulity that colored her voice.

"You have the same aura." She gave Lydia a smile that made her feel warm all over. "Your Mamá Juanita and I are old friends, although I haven't seen her in many years. She moved to Mexicali shortly after she married. How is she?"

"Oh, she's very well, *gracias*." She hesitated. "She's the one who suggested I come to see you."

"Then come in to your house." Doña Tichi anointed her with the aromatic smoke and opened the gate. Lydia followed the sorceress to a small table under a flowering *sauco* tree. "Will you have tea with me? It's already made."

They sat together sipping their tea without words until Doña Tichi asked, "Now tell me why you think your life is in jeopardy."

Lydia needed no further credentials and over a cup of *pasiflora* tea she explained that Fermin was in danger any time he got behind the wheel of a car. "I fear for his life as well as for my own."

"Yes, I understand perfectly. I will need several things from you. I will need a piece of your husband's clothing and a small amount of his hair. The rest of the *santería* is up to me."

"I can have these things back here this afternoon."

"Good. These charms can only be performed during a growing moon or will not meet with success. We are very fortunate that the moon is just now coming full."

That same afternoon Lydia returned with one of Fermin's old shirts, his hairbrush provided the rest of the material. Doña Tichi accepted them and told her to return the following day.

Lydia was back as soon as Fermin left for the office. "I have your *santería* all ready for you, my dear," Doña Tichi said as she anointed her with incense smoke. She handed Lydia a crude looking doll shaped from a corncob and aromatic twigs dressed in Fermin's shirt. She saw a small nest of her husband's black hair bound to the doll with red silk thread. The strange little figure appeared to have been soaked in something and had the pleasant smell of an herbal sachet.

Lydia held the crude little figure in her hands, her eyes filling with tears. And yet she did not feel the least bit sad.

"It is the energy that moves you, my dear, yours is a natural reaction. All you need do is place this amulet somewhere in your husband's car where no one is likely to find it. Someone might not understand its purpose and throw it out."

"That's all there is to it?"

"I know what you're thinking, my dear, this is all perfect nonsense." Doña Tichi didn't want to give Lydia time to become embarrassed for her thoughts. "No one in the car will ever die while this *santería* is in place. Never. Simple, no?"

Lydia reached for her purse but the little sorceress stopped her. "I cannot charge you for this. If you feel generous put your gift in that hollow gourd and go in God's company."

Lydia pulled out a two hundred-peso note and deposited it in the gourd. Doña Tichi gave her a warm embrace and Lydia headed for her car. She drove off with a strange but pleasant feeling of spiritual refreshment. She was astonished that such powerful magic could be bought for two hundred pesos. If it really worked it was priceless!

That same day Fermin came home early, exhausted, and complaining of the flu.

"You don't have the flu, hangover is more like it."

"Please!" Fermin was not prepared for the indictment and had no desire to testify on his own behalf. Especially when he didn't have a case.

"You got in at twenty minutes to three this morning. Where were you?"

Fermin elected to affect grief. It worked before. "Poor old Balderas. I had to go to his rosary last night. I forgot to tell you. I'm sorry."

"Poor old Balderas."

"Yes, he wasn't that old."

"YOU BURIED BALDERAS LAST WEEK!"

Fermin had no option but to try to salvage the moment with another lie. "That was his uncle." I'm going to have to be a lot more careful next time, he thought. This woman does not let hair grow on her tongue!

Lydia relaxed her hostility and opened the bed so he could lie down for a siesta. Seizing opportunity, she grabbed his keys from the kitchen counter where he habitually emptied his pockets when he got home, and ran to his car. In the trunk she found a can of Mobile 1 motor oil, a towel, a suspicious-looking blanket, and a pair of pantyhose that were not hers. Unfortunately this was inadmissible evidence. If she confronted him he would be sure to clean out the trunk and discover the amulet. She left everything exactly as she had found it and hid the little charm under the spare tire. When she got back to the house she was trembling and fixed herself a cup of chocolate.

It was a couple of months later when Fermin was returning from a new conquest on the beach in Ensenada that turned out to be far more successful that his misadventure with Susi. Mimi was a local girl he met in a lobster house some months back. The nude scene on the silver-plated beach was a resounding success. Somewhere around two or three in the morning he took her home and started for Tecate. There was no one on the road, no witnesses to what happened so most of the following can only be regarded as speculation. The weather was clear, the road, while never in acceptable condition, was at least dry. He may have swerved to avoid a collision with a cow, another vehicle could have crossed into his lane. Or he could have dozed for a second. No one will ever know for sure. For whatever reason Fermin failed to negotiate the tight curve just before the descent into Valle de las Palmas. The car plunged down a hundred foot embankment, and landed upside-down. It was crushed like an egg. Moments later the cadmium orange Camaro exploded in flames.

That night was a living nightmare for Lydia. Sleep was out of the question. She scoured her mind for the darkest thoughts then nourished them into the worst scenario. Fermin was lying dead somewhere. Of that she was certain. She was up every few minutes to check the clock, to pace the house, and answer the demands of the bladder. It was not unusual for Fermin to stay out late. But he always came home. Dawn was beginning to light the gray edges of the morning. She was furious. She was livid. She was frightened. She looked out the window and into the street. Nothing. She began to prepare the screed she was going to lay on him the moment he came through that door.

The ring of the doorbell door paralyzed her. Her blood turned to ice. She couldn't bring herself to answer it. She knew who it was. A policeman from Federal de Caminos would be standing there to tell her that her husband was killed on the highway. She didn't want to hear it. If it was Fermin he wouldn't stand out there ringing the bell. The authority of the second ring was a command. She opened it to a massive man in the green uniform of Federal de Caminos. She was sure she would faint and gripped the door with both hands until the dizzy spell passed.

That's when she saw Fermin standing slightly behind the officer. She was going to throttle him. "Just what do you think you're doing getting here at this — Oh my God! — darling, are your hurt, are you all right? What happened to you?" She flew to him, wrapped her arms around him, and covered him with kisses. "I thought I would never see you again and —" she burst into inconsolable tears.

"Nothing serious, *mi amor*, it's all right." Fermin was still too shaky to say more.

The policeman spoke. "His car went over a cliff at kilometer thirty, señora, burst into flames, and the man walks away. Something of a miracle I would say."

The officer helped Lydia get Fermin to the sofa and left. Lydia was out of her mind and wasn't even sure if she had thanked him. She was numb with fear and relief and fury all at once. Then she threw herself into her husband's arms and surrendered to tears of anger and gratitude. Part of her wanted to scream at him. Instead she thanked God for his safe return and made the cross. When she began to regain her senses, she thought of a little Indian witch and a corncob doll dressed in her husband's shirt. Lydia decanted all her remaining tears.

Fermin was too stiff and achy to go to work. Lydia waited on her lord hand and foot. She sat him in his easy chair in front of the television, lovingly made him all the things he loved to eat, and brought them to him with a kiss. She rubbed his back with lotion. Lydia did not scold, made no inquiries, no accusations. Fermin stayed home and enjoyed the pampering he was receiving. But by the third day he became restless. He took Lydia's car and went to the office. His car was covered by his own company, of course. He would get a new one next week. Maybe a Pontiac Firebird this time. Red would be nice.

Lydia had a lot to think about. She almost lost the man she loved. Whatever his faults she could never stop loving him. As soon as she saw the car pull away she called her grandmother in Mexicali.

"It's a miracle Mamá Juanita, nothing less than a miracle. He walked away with cuts and bruises. He's quite stiff and sore, but he's alive." The thought made Lydia's eyes burn with fresh tears. "If you hadn't told me about Doña Tichi he would be dead."

"I would like to have a word with him."

"He insisted on going back to the office this morning."

"And just what was he doing returning from Ensenada at three in the morning?"

"Pinning the horns on me! I didn't want it to be true. My heart is in pieces, Mamacita, but I still love him. A broken heart is without pride." She burst into tears. "I just don't know how to deal with it!"

"The same way all women have dealt with it over the centuries. Mice in the pantry. As long as he is good to you, it is best to ignore it. Why put your hand in the flames?"

Once again Fermin found himself in Dr. Bolaños' examining room. He sat on the table in his underwear. "You were very lucky,

Fermin. It's a miracle you're alive. It is almost as though someone was watching over you."

Fermin was not in any mood to encourage conversation. He was too sore and too achy to listen to a lecture today. He just wanted out. "I hurt from head to foot."

"Of course you do! The whiplash. But I've seen the x-rays, there are no broken bones. I see no evidence of internal injuries. Miraculous! But I want to take some blood and urine, and do a number of other tests. I'll give you something for pain."

Fermin came down off the examining table with caution and began to get dressed. He ached all over.

"I want to see you here a week from today."

It was a long miserable week for Fermin. Not one, but two, *two*, sexy *chamacas* he'd been pursuing called and left word with his office to have him return the call. Damn! Why couldn't they have called last week?

He speculated for a moment on what fantastic things he could have done with either of them just a few days ago. But this was today and while he couldn't accept it, he knew he was in no condition to pursue the rites of the flesh. He still could not move without pain. Every part of his body was stiff with one notable exception.

Remarkably, on the appointed day a week later, Fermin had lost a lot of the stiffness and pain when he walked in to Dr. Bolaños' office.

"How are you feeling?"

"Much improved, doctor. I can move my legs and arms much better. My back is less stiff. And look, I can actually turn my head now without pain."

"Good, good, I'm pleased. But I have some very disturbing news for you, I'm afraid." Dr. Bolaños opened his medical folder, shuffled through the growing file, and withdrew a laboratory report.

Ay, ay, ay! Here it comes, Fermin lamented. I'm going to have to listen to my cholesterol numbers and sit through his damn lecture again. I'm just not in the mood for it today. Well, I'll stop him cold. "I know, I know, the cholesterol thing. I promise you strict adherence to your instructions. And I promise to bring you all good numbers on my next visit." Fermin made his move toward the door.

"No, no, it isn't that, Fermin. I want you to look at this laboratory report. You've been infected with AIDS."

The Cafeteros suspended breathing. The only sound was the timid clink of cups and saucers. La Fonda was still without electric power. The candles on our table were low now and shivered in their sockets. The melancholy rain continued its dismal drumming. Our poet/accountant put down his coffee and went to lay another log on the fire. He answered my question before I could ask it.

"After uprooting lives and ravaging Tecate, Hurricane Fermin headed south, leaving behind a grim swath of human destruction and broken hearts in its wake."

The Last Furlong

"*Tsi, tsi.* It appears they are going to recall the governor of California," the medico said, putting down the Friday morning edition of the *San Diego Union-Tribune.* The Cafeteros, our Upper Chamber of Deputies, were gathered around the coffee pot at their morning table at La Fonda as was their usual custom.

"Yes, I understand they want to put in that movie star with an unpronounceable name," El Ranchero said.

"You mean Schw— Schwa—" That was as far as the shoe merchant could get.

"Don't even try it," warned our dentist "You could do irreparable injury to your tongue."

"He's right," agreed the banker. "I have a *compadre* who thinks he's Big Señor Linguist, and in the attempt to articulate the actor's name, he dislocated his jaw."

"I don't think we've ever recalled a governor," the medico observed.

"Just presidents." El Ranchero said.

"Who was the last president we recalled?"

"Obregon. In 1928," answered the *licenciado* who knows all the dates and places in Mexican history. "And by only four votes."

"But that was enough," our poet/accountant said. "Those were .38 caliber votes."

"How can a restaurant serve lethal dishes to its patrons and stay in business? I don't understand it," the banker said to anyone who might be listening, thus bringing the topic of politics to a close. The subject matter up for discussion among the Cafeteros is seldom of great duration. The banker was now browsing through the medico's newspaper. "This review will ruin El Rancho Grande Mexican Cafe in Old Town in San Diego."

The merchant caught the question and answered with another. "Dear friend and esteemed colleague, what *are* you talking about?"

"I am reading a restaurant review. And the reviewer says that El Rancho Grande Mexican Cafe serves killer enchiladas. I swear I'm not making this up."

"It's an American idiomatic expression," our poet/accountant explained.

"What a strange language."

"I've heard a beautiful woman described as 'drop-dead gorgeous.' Can you imagine such a thing?"

Another sudden shift in theme brought them to the subject of movies. "Has anyone seen the new film, *Seabiscuit*?" the poet/accountant inquired. "We saw it last night. What a beautiful story!"

"Indeed, the horse is a noble beast," agreed El Ranchero and refilled his cup.

"He can be," the *licenciado* corrected. "But the *caballo* can also be a treacherous animal."

The ranchero put down his coffee to address the new subject. "I've known horses to be stubborn, I've known horses that will happily buck you off. But treacherous?"

The *licenciado* took the Gerber jar with the holes in the lid and poured sugar into his coffee. "Then let me tell you the story of my cousin Alvaro."

Cousin Alvaro and his young wife, Alicia, labored long and hard on their little rancho in Cerro Azul (the *licenciado* began) and they lived well, though owing to the uncertainties of farming, they had to be thrifty.

It was their custom to sit out on the front porch in the evening when the chores of the day were done by virtue of darkness, as they're never really done on a rancho. It was their special nightly ritual for the three years they'd been married. It gave them a few minutes every evening to be close together. Alicia brought Alvaro a cold beer and sat next to him on the steps. They listened to the night noises, clicking, croaking, chirping, and the final scuffle of the little creatures as they made ready for bed. They watched the fireworks show provided by the fireflies.

"I remember when I was a little girl we would run out and gather the *lucérnagas* and pin them to our dresses and pretend we were a princess."

"When we were kids we used to race stink bugs."

"How could you touch those repulsive things? And how on earth could you race them?"

"We drew a circle in the dirt then we would all put our bug in the center. The first one to crawl out of the circle was the winner." Alvaro loved the music of Alicia's laughter when he related anecdotes of his childhood. "But I gave it up. I always lost all the money I had saved up for candy."

Alicia laughed again. "Maybe that was a good thing. You don't gamble."

There was fluttering in the oak trees and they heard the first mournful hoots of the owls complaining to the moon.

Tu-whoo, tu-whoo.

Alicia looked out into the night. "It was fun to play outdoors in the dark. But then as soon as my grandmother heard the owls she would hurry us in the house, and of course, to bed."

"She was afraid of owls?"

"You know the old superstition: the owl is the incarnation of someone who died."

"I've heard it all my life."

"By the way," Alicia asked. "Are we going to see our *compadres* tomorrow? I have a big box of clothes for them."

"I expect we will. I have a load of vegetables in the truck and a box of eggs."

Alicia got up and rubbed his shoulder affectionately. "Don't stay out too late, *mi amor*, I'm going to bed."

"Afraid of the owl?"

Alicia laughed and the screen door slammed behind her. Alvaro sipped the cold fizzy beverage and his thoughts turned to his poor *compadres*.

Narciso and Virginia were perennially destitute. There was never enough money for the barest necessities. They lived in two rooms with a bare concrete floor. Virginia owned one dress, their two-year-old, Carlitos, had few clothes and his only toys were pot lids and a rubber sink plunger. They sustained themselves every day on beans and rice that, by virtue of Virginia's alchemy at the kitchen stove, pleased the palate and filled the empty spaces of the body.

It wasn't that Narciso didn't work hard. He laid brick for a living. The work was arduous. He earned more than enough for he and his family to live decently. And he was never short of work — just money. Narciso's problem was that he suffered from a terminal case of equineuxoria, a viral infection that remains dormant in the nervous system until the horses are at the gate. This was accompanied by a high fever that put Narciso in a state of chronic drought. He was presently undergoing treatment at the Caliente, Tecate's only booking parlor. There he would absorb a few beers, and lay a bet on a horse he knew would spread his wings, and like Pegasus, fly to victory. Then came the vision. When the horses turned for home, he could already see himself bursting through the front door and strewing gold pieces at Virginia's feet. He would dance her around the room and she would throw her arms around him, splashing him with tears of joy!

Then he would go home and face the *música*.

Narciso picked up the virus in all innocence. One day he accompanied a friend to the booking parlor who wanted to place a bet on the Dallas Cowboys against Green Bay. For something to do while he waited, Narciso casually put fifty pesos on La Llorona. He came home with five hundred pesos and the infection.

"What a cute little suit!" Virginia exclaimed, holding up a little jacket of navy blue with bright brass buttons, red trim on collar and pockets, and a matching pair of short pants.

"I thought it would look so nice on Carlitos," Alicia said.

The two *comadres* were unpacking a carton of used clothing in Virginia's bedroom. Little Carlitos was fast asleep in his crib, consisting of some old sofa cushions arranged on the floor. The house was dark at eleven in the morning as the government-owned power company had cut off their electricity for non-payment the day before yesterday. The house had only two other rooms, a kitchen equipped with a two-burner stove nourished by a butane cylinder, and a bathroom with a cantankerous toilet that would regurgitate violently when an innocent passenger was least expecting it. The basin and tub still hadn't been connected but there was a big galvanized bucket in the room for bathing and laundry. The two husbands had already unloaded cartons of squash, corn, freshly picked tomatoes and eggs, then went off somewhere to quench their thirst.

Alicia pulled out a cheery yellow dress with an attached belt. "I thought this would look better on you than on me. I'm getting so fat!" It was a lie but she didn't want to embarrass her *comadre* any more than she already was at these weekly acts of charity. Virginia was dressed in a Sea World T-shirt with a hole in the armpit, blue jeans with a see-through seat, and a pair of plastic sandals. Her dark hair was limp and her eyes too sad for a girl of twenty. She wore the unmistakable pallor of poverty on her youthful face.

"*Gracias, comadre.* We'll make good use of all this. Come to the kitchen I'll put on the coffee pot." Virginia sent up a quick prayer asking that there would be coffee in the tin and gas in the cylinder.

"Bartender, one more beer over here!"

"No, no, Narciso, we've had enough," Alvaro pleaded. "We better get home before our wives get angry and put us to the boil like beans." They were sitting in La Cucaracha, a cantina popular with laborers in need of a restorative and sometimes the companionship of the other sex if they weren't too selective.

The two beers arrived. "This will be the last one," promised Narciso. "I almost had a winner yesterday. And I would be all set for the week. I was going to buy Virginia a new pair of shoes and one of those little battery-operated toy cars for Carlitos." He sucked on the amber bottle like a hungry baby at his mother's breast. "I work hard for my family," he said with a tone of heroism in his voice. "I don't want anything for myself. Family first!"

"I could never afford to gamble, *compadre*," Alvaro said. "It's hard enough to get by without throwing the money away."

"I wasn't throwing it away, *compadre*, I came that close — that close!" He held up thumb and forefinger within a centimeter of each other to demonstrate how close he'd come to winning a sack of gold. "Next time I'll hit it big, *compa*, and you know the first thing I'm going to do?"

Yes, you'll throw it away, Alvaro thought.

"I'm going to finish the house!" He slapped the bar to punctuate his admirable intention. "Virginia deserves a nice house. And Carlitos needs a bed. I'll get him one of those little beds with all the pretty pictures of bears in their pajamas. Carlitos will like that." Narciso brought a handkerchief to his face and wiped his eyes. "I love my family, *compa*. They are my reason for getting up in the morning."

As usual, Alvaro paid for the beers and dragged him back to his house. They found their wives gossiping over a cup of coffee. Carlitos sat on Alicia's lap playing with a set of keys. The men declined Virginia's offer of coffee, one because he suspected there was no more, the other because he knew. They joined them in idle chatter in the gloomy kitchen.

"I just don't know what our government is coming to," Narciso barked to cover his guilt. "I paid the light bill two days ago and the *cabrones* turn off the power. Tomorrow I go to the Comisión and complain." Everyone in the kitchen knew he was lying.

"By the way," Virginia said, "if you want dinner you will have to go down to the gas company and get a new cylinder. We're out of gas."

"I'm sorry, *mi amor*, it's all my fault. I should have thought of it earlier," Narciso answered in all sincerity. "I'll go right now, *corazón*, right now!" Narciso started toward the door. "Keep me company, *compadre*?"

Alvaro knew it wasn't so much his company that was needed as it was the three hundred pesos for a cylinder of butane. They ran the errand and hooked up the gas.

"You'll stay for dinner?" Narciso asked.

"*Gracias*, we can't stay. I have to get back and feed the animals," Alvaro said. They all exchanged warm *abrazos*, kissed the baby, and Alvaro and Alicia started for home.

"I know he's my *compadre*," Alicia said as the old pickup rumbled down the pitted highway on their way home. "But I get so mad at him I could strangle him! How can he let his family live like that? The baby sleeps on the floor, no lights, no gas! I don't dare use the bathroom while we're there. You and Narciso just go outside, but a woman isn't equally equipped."

"Maybe that's a good thing."

Alicia slapped him playfully on the thigh and continued her theme. "If we didn't bring a box of old clothes and food from the rancho every week they would be in rags and starve."

"I know," Alvaro answered in a voice gray as the sky in February. "It's a sickness. The man earns good money but he just can't stop gambling. I'm glad I've never done that. Maybe one day he'll see what he's doing and look after his family."

But Narciso had a blind spot. He could never see what he was doing to his family. He also didn't see the big Pan Bimbo bread truck rumbling in his direction when he stepped into the intersection against a red light on his way to the Caliente with golden dreams dancing in his head.

The day of the funeral Alvaro and Alicia came home exhausted. The Mass and the burial and the statutory reunion at the new widow's home were emotionally draining. Everyone took a turn at weeping and comforting the inconsolable Virginia. There was no room for so many people in the miserable little house. They sat outdoors eating the vast donations of food without appetite. Even the tequila with fresh lemon and salt didn't taste the same as it did when the occasion was festive.

As soon as they were home Alvaro changed his clothes and went out to attend to his cows and pigs and the two goats that were eating their way out of their pen. He would have to turn them into barbecue soon before they chewed the wood enclosure to sawdust. Alicia saw to the chickens then went to do those things in the house that demand doing in perpetuity.

Late that evening they sat out on the front porch as they did every night. They needed the moment together. Alicia brought Alvaro a cold beer and sat down next to him on the steps. They watched the mysteries of the universe, a crown of gold under a veil studded with sparkling diamonds. They didn't talk, just sat and listened to the voices of the night. The tree toads croaked the same old song they provided every night, the crickets answered with the second verse. Their neighbor's dogs were barking at a rabbit they must have cornered, and far away behind the hill, they could hear the coyotes were having a party. The plaintive hoot of a lone owl came to them from somewhere in the darkness.

Tu-whoo, tu-whoo.

"I feel so sad about my *compadre*," Alvaro sighed. "He had a good heart."

"I do too. But I'm sorrier for my *comadre*, and Carlitos. I don't know how she's going to manage."

"It's going to be hard for Virginia."

"Every night I thank God that you're not a gambler and a womanizer. I would leave you if you were." Her voice sounded mournful as the whistle of a night train in the distance. "We have to save for every little thing we need, clothes, furniture, everything. One day we'll have enough for that used tractor you need so badly."

"Or a new washing machine," Alvaro said. "The one you have won't survive another load."

"I don't mind scrimping and saving for the things we need."

Alvaro put a hand on her knee. I am so fortunate, he told himself, to have such a good woman at my side. Marrying her was the smartest thing I ever did in my life.

"You've always been a good and trustworthy man," Alicia continued, "and that's probably why sometimes I forget to tell you I love you."

Alvaro couldn't answer. He wiped his eyes and put the cold bottle to his lips.

"I'm not one of those stupid women who can't appreciate what they have until after they lose it. Might as well never have it!"

They sat a little while longer before Alicia got up to go inside. "It's getting cool. Don't stay out here too late." She touched his shoulder and went inside the house.

Alvaro remained contemplating Life's unanswered questions. Why are some poor while others have everything? Why do some grow old and others die young? Why did God take our first baby before he was born? Will we have another chance?

He put the empty beer bottle down and watched a big brown owl flutter down and perch on the oak tree just off the porch.

Tu-whoo, tu-whoo.

Alvaro looked into a pair of big yellow eyes. They blinked at him. He contemplated the creature for a moment, yawned, and started for the door.

"Pssst! *Compadre.*"

Alvaro spun around and nearly fell off the porch. The voice sounded just like his *compadre.* There was no one out there. He knew he was hallucinating. The funeral was too much for him, that's what it was, an emotional strain. He loved his *compadre.* It was definitely time for bed. Once again he turned to go.

"Pssstt! *Compadre.* Don't go!"

"Crazy owl!" he shouted. "Go away. Find another tree."

"*Compadre.* It's me!"

"Then go in the barn and eat the mice!" Once more Alvaro turned to go.

"*Compadre* — don't go — it's *me!*"

Like every Mexican Alvaro grew up steeped in legends and superstitions. As a child he heard eerie tales of the spirit world that kept him awake at night, first from his grandmother then his parents, his uncles and cousins — everyone had a story of a relative who died and came back in the form of an owl. He could never bring himself to believe such a thing. But right now he couldn't quite disbelieve it. It was unmistakably Narciso's voice.

"Is that — is that really you, *compadre?*" he said mostly to himself. He did not expect an answer.

"Of course, it's me! I'm only in the ground for a day and you've already forgotten me?"

"I can never forget you, *compadre.*" Now I know I'm going crazy. I'm talking to an owl! "What — what do you want?"

"I know the winner of the last race at the Hipódromo."

"What are you talking about?"

"I want you to go to the Caliente and place a bet for me on La Malinche."

"You and I have had some good times together, *compa.* But you know I've never gambled in my life. I work too hard for my money to throw it away."

"Just this once, *compa.* Do it for me."

Alvaro didn't answer. He ran into the house and jumped in bed beside his wife.

"I thought I heard voices, were you talking to someone?"

"No!" Alvaro put an arm around his wife and pulled her closer. "Go to sleep, *mi amor.*"

Tu-whoo, tu-whoo.

These unwanted visits from the owl continued for several nights and Alvaro couldn't take any more. He suggested they sit out back in the evenings, but Alicia wasn't keen on the idea. There was really no comfortable place to sit out back. She liked the front porch where they could get the cool air from the west.

Alvaro acquiesced and every night he and Alicia continued to sit on the porch and hold hands as they always did. It was one of the few moments of a busy day they had together. They talked softly about various things, the newborn calf, the melons he would take to market, the baby they both wanted. Alicia brought him his beer and they sat quietly listening to the crickets scratching the air like untuned violins. Frogs down by the creek were croaking their symphony under the stars. The earth smelled dark and rich and fertile. It was their favorite time of day. But tonight Alvaro wasn't saying much.

"What is it, *mi amor*, you're so quiet?"

"I don't know." He wasn't going to tell her that the damn owl came and talked to him every night after she went inside. She would think he was crazy. Maybe he *was* crazy.

"Are you worried about something? Tell me." Alicia rubbed his thigh. "I knew when I married you that a farmer takes God for a partner. There are frosts and droughts and pestilence — all sorts of things that can damage a crop. But I want you to know, I trust Him and I trust you. Blindly."

Alvaro answered with an arm around her shoulder. "I know, *mi amor*, I know."

"I know what's wrong with you. You haven't been sleeping properly. Every night I can feel you doing cartwheels in bed. And you're nervous. You've been jumpy as a mouse in the grain bin."

Alvaro made no reply.

"Last night I heard cats fighting outside our window and when I got up I realized the noises were coming from your stomach! It's Narciso that has you worried, isn't it?"

Not Narcisco, he thought. The owl! But he didn't say anything.

"Well, there is nothing you can do for him. It's Virginia we have to think about now."

"I suppose you're right."

And that night, soon after Alicia went inside, the miserable owl was back!

Tu-whoo, tu-whoo.

Alvaro couldn't take anymore. "No! Please, owl, please. I beg! Go away."

Tu-whoo, tu-whoo.

"Ay *compa*! One simple little bet. Do it for *me*."

"No."

"Then do it for Virginia."

The owl struck a nerve.

"Look, just this once. Place a bet on La Malinche. It's money in the bank! Just this once *compa*, and I promise not to come back."

Anything was worth getting rid of the cursed owl. "You promise?"

"I promise!"

"Win or lose, you don't come back."

"*Palabra!*"

The very next day while Alicia went to the hardware store Alvaro prepared to make a withdrawal from their secret unnumbered account. He slipped into their bedroom and pulled the dresser away from the wall. There, in the hollow he created when he removed an adobe, reposed the family treasury, each dusty bank note mute evidence of something they did without. With trembling hands he took ten thousand pesos and replaced the dresser exactly as it was. He felt like a thief. It's not a risk I'm taking, he told himself, I'm going to lose it. All of it. It's all we have. Alicia will get mad and she'll cry when she finds out what I've done. Worst of all, I'll lose her trust.

But that owl is driving me insane. Peace at any price! I will cross *el Rubicón* with stout heart and bold spirit. I'll face up to my deed and Doña Fortuna. Dear God, I promise I will find a way to make it up to her.

The *licenciado* had everyone at the table clinging to his every word.

Everyone put down their coffee and looked to the narrator for footnotes and epilogue. Our poet/accountant was the first to speak. "And what happened to Alvaro? Did he really do it?"

The *licenciado*, a born showman, prolonged his audience's agony. He leisurely refilled his cup, added sugar, slowly poured a trickle of milk into it, and stirred. "Yes," he said at last. "My cousin Alvaro went to the Caliente, and with tears in his eyes, placed his life's savings on La Malinche, a hopeless jughead that closed at a hundred and eight to one."

A prodigious silence fell over Los Cafeteros. It is a rare event indeed for these men to find themselves incapable of speech.

The merchant broke the silence in a low whisper. "And the owl never came back?"

"The owl never came back," echoed the *licenciado*.

"What an incredible story!"

"And, of course, La Malinche betrayed him at the finish line and he lost everything," El Ranchero said. "That was the whole point of your story, no? Does the story end there?"

"No." The *licenciado* had every Cafetero's attention again.

"Then what?" They all demanded at once.

"Go to his rancho in Cerro Azul. You'll see my cousin Alvaro disking his fields with a John Deere." The *licenciado*, who as usual was running a little late, finished off his coffee and got to his feet. "And their *comadre* had the house finished, Carlitos got a real bed with pictures of little bears in their pajamas, and for the first time in her life, Virginia has money in the bank."

Big Caca's Revenge

A number of years have passed since the events that follow took place. And yet, the scar remains. We had a terrorist lurking in Tecate. Time has failed to erase the memory. You can still hear the locals talking about *el terrorista* with residual fear coloring their voices. In the cantinas, the cafes, in the plaza. Sometimes, while waiting for the light to turn red to get safely across our only avenue, I can hear little snatches of conversation, and the dreaded name is whispered, a name that can still send goosy chills down all twenty-four vertebrae of the spinal column — Big Caca.

Big Caca is as despicable a man as ever broke tortilla and despised with a passion. This dreaded individual is the commander at the border. He alone decides what can come into Mexico from the U.S. and what cannot. He is not awash with the milk of human kindness and no one has ever seen a rainbow round his shoulder. One day when golden sunbeams fell on Tecate and all was right with the world, I came through the border in my usual high spirits. Someone once said, I forget who, power corrupts and absolute power corrupts absolutely. Meet Señor Absolute Power. Big Caca writes legislation as needed and sets importation fees on the spot. He found a six-pack of petunias I picked up at Garden Town Nursery in San Diego and immediately threatened to confiscate my car. The petunias cost me a buck. But I got to keep my car.

In pursuit of Truth I'm obliged to tell you that he was never officially baptized Big Caca by the local padre. His real name was Ismael Cacabelos. He was built low to the ground. What I believe is called the center of gravity was buried in that massive gluteal region we call *nalgas*. The fit of his olive green uniform was a disgrace to his office, but the .45 on his hip swelled the brass buttons on his bosom with pride and importance. He weighed more than a small car. But inside that enormous exterior, we knew there was a tyrant trying to get out. When you looked into his face you would logically conclude that you were looking at an eggplant with a mustache and a wart on the left nostril. In short, Big Caca was a frontal assault on the optic nerve.

The man himself seemed unaware of his physical disadvantage. He considered himself a ladies' man and was perennially in pursuit of that endeavor. This may have been due to some undiagnosed mental disorder. He often trolled the plaza for candidates and one day saw a woman of extraordinary beauty he'd never seen before. She was slim where slimness was preferred and bountiful where bountiful was desirable. She was dressed in shimmering turquoise pants and matching jacket that fitted her like the skin on a mango. Big Caca held his breath and missed a heartbeat. He inquired as to her identity and learned her name was Lizette. Lizette became an obsession.

It is said in town that he made daily prayers and lit candles in hopes the beautiful Lizette would one day come through the gate, something like a black widow who waits for a victim to get tangled in its web. But his supplications to divine deities were not answered. It had been weeks since his first sighting of the apparition in the plaza. He was on the edge of abandoning hope. Then one ripe summer day Doña Fortuna, as Fate so often does, delivered that something into his web.

Big Caca stood at the border extorting fees in the name of the law as usual. It was a slow day. It was nearly two in the afternoon and nothing much was coming through. A pickup truck with a used washing machine came in and that was good for twenty American dollars but he could tell it was going to be a dismal day. He looked up at the next car in line. A white Volkswagen. Not much there, he thought, when he saw the woman at the wheel.

Lizette!

Lizette was returning from a day of heavy shopping at the wholesale showrooms in the garment district in San Diego. She did this often. But not for herself. She shopped for her clients, ladies who didn't have time or didn't have the proper papers to cross the border. It was a business. A highly profitable business. She always brought back several hundred dollars worth of women's apparel and never paid bribe or duty. She made it a point to cross the border late at night when the sleepy officer would be sipping coffee in the little guardhouse watching the late night show, and he would just wave her through. If she just had the right connection, she thought, she could enter Mexico with most of Macy's inventory and not get fleeced. But she didn't have the right connection and when she saw the eggplant with all the brass buttons and the glimmering badge of authority she knew she was going to get hit pretty hard. She always did her best to avoid him but she knew who he was.

"*Buenas tardes*, señorita," he oozed. "What do you have to declare?"

"*Buenas tardes*, Comandante," she answered melodically in metrical cadence, as though reciting a lyric poem. "Only a few items of clothing for my personal use."

Big Caca walked officiously around to the other door and began to grope through the contraband. He found dresses, skirts and blouses. Upon further snooping he found at least twenty pairs of panties in a variety of colors and bras to match. He held up a shimmering black Playtex underwire bra designed to separate and lift, then the matching black panties no larger than a cocktail napkin.

"And all this is for your personal use, señorita?"

"A girl never has enough underwear, you know."

"What you have here, señorita, comes close to seven hundred dollars in duty."

Any other girl would have thought all was lost. But not our beautiful Lizette. She took the bra he was fondling and held it up to herself. "What if I just keep this one?" Before he could find words she reached in the bag and withdrew a Playtex "Barely

There" creation in ripe plum with front closure. "Or this? Which one do you think looks best on me?" She watched the eyes in the eggplant swell to the size of ping-pong balls. "I'd like to keep the matching *calzones* you presently hold in your hand. I can return the rest. Would that be all right?"

Big Caca ogled the bra she was holding to her bosom and fingered the slinky garment in his hand. "Look, señorita, we are here to control the borders of our sovereign nation, not to discommode nice people. Why don't you meet me for a drink at La Fonda this evening. Seven, say?"

Lizette had found that important connection she needed to stay in business. "Seven it is," she sang, and the Volkswagen rumbled into Mexico.

Now, the story circulating around Tecate has several versions. We must accept the fact that a small portion of this drama is pure conjecture as there were no witnesses. But I will identify these passages in the interest of honest reporting.

The affair between the comandante and Lizette was both romantic and symmetrical. Big Caca got to play *nalgas*, and Lizette could drive into Mexico with an armed missile if she so desired. As promised, the following scenes are conjecture because only the two of them were present when it happened.

One pleasant day in June Big Caca invited Lizette for a weekend in the country. They crossed the border into the U.S. early in the morning and were soon in Temecula, a picturesque wine-growing village in San Diego County. It is bucolic and quiet, claims the most spectacular sunsets in the county, and produces some fine wines that win high praise from those who know good wine when it rolls on the discerning tongue.

The happy couple registered at the Chardonnay Inn, a bed and breakfast in a pretty garden setting not far from the vineyards. Big Caca was more interested in the first B than the second, but he agreed with Lizette that a walk along a quiet lane was the ideal way to say adios to the day. He was dressed in a pair of baggy cotton pants and a Mexican guayabera blouse. He felt naked without his uniform, the gleaming emblem of authority on his breast, and the .45 to back it up. But those articles of his authority had to stay in Mexico. Lizette was in ratty blue jeans and shirt. But in all probability her underwear was exquisite. They both wore sandals. "I always think of the sunset as the sun's final farewell before slain by the night. It is as sad as it is beautiful," Lizette recited in a romantic whisper.

Big Caca was not a poet. The red sunset reminded him of *huevos rancheros*. He garbled something in his throat and Lizette took this to mean that he was too overcome with emotion to express his innermost thoughts about the sunset. They joined hands and stood among the grapevines until the last light expired. Big Caca could feel the effects of the Viagra he'd taken earlier and was looking forward to nightfall and the B.

A red and blue light flashed behind them. Big Caca thought maybe it was part of the celestial phenomena at sundown. It wasn't. It was a white station wagon with a cage in the back. The U.S. Border Patrol.

The grim-looking officer in forest green uniform stood eight-two at the very least and didn't give the impression he was the type who cared much for natural spectacles in the heavens. He swaggered up to Big Caca.

"Citizenship," he demanded. It wasn't a question. Big Caca reached for his wallet while the Border Patrol reached for his pistol but didn't draw. Seeing everything was legal he gave the papers back. "Okay Hosay, no *problema*." Big Caca bristled at the disrespect. "Now, yours," he said looking at Lizette.

"My purse is back at the inn!"

"Sure it is. You won't be picking grapes tomorrow, señorita. Come along and take a ride with me. I'll get you back to your own country and we won't have no problems."

Big Caca nearly exploded. A few miles south of where he now stood, and just across a four-strand barbed wire fence, he had the authority to make mincemeat out of this big stupid *cabron* and he was being taken for a common grape picker! He began to protest in badly frayed English.

"You just stay right there, Hosay," the Jolly Green Giant said in a voice Big Caca recognized as dangerous.

Big Caca quickly realized he was outside his sphere of power. If he challenged the officer he would most likely radio for a back-up and haul his *nalgas* away too. He swallowed his humiliation in livid silence.

"Don't be upset, *mi amor.* Condemn the law, not its agent," Lizette said in her sweet poetic voice. "He is only performing his duty."

Big Caca stood and watched impotently as his beautiful Lizette was put in the cage and driven away like a rabid dog. "Duty!" he spat as the wagon disappeared. "I'll show you duty!" Big Caca was no philosopher, and as we saw earlier, he did not have the heart of a poet. He watched the Border Patrol disappear over the crest of the road and the burning fire of vengeance was already smoldering in his bowels.

The foregoing scene ends the portion of surmise I alluded to earlier. Now we can proceed to the area of reality. We have reliable witnesses for everything that follows.

Big Caca's revenge began the very next day.

We were standing at the bar of the Diana saloon named in honor of the famous huntress whose portrait dominates the back bar. The deity of the hunt was watching us from her position. She must have left all her clothes somewhere in the forest for she was stark naked, back arched, muscles tense, as she prepared to release an arrow from her oaken bow. Mario the bartender was practicing his alchemy with tequila and limes in the blender. There was the banker, two lawyers, and Jerry, an American who owned a big factory that employed a hundred workers. And there was Chavez the dentist who hopefully had no appointments this afternoon. It was a friendly group of regulars. We all knew each other over a period of many years. A trio consisting of guitar, accordion, and bass viol provided jumpy little tunes that added to the conviviality.

The sudden dimming of the bright daylight from outside announced an addition to our party had just entered through the door. There was a total eclipse. We all turned toward the door as one to see who had come to raise a glass with us and the place fell silent as Moctezuma's tomb. Laughter froze in the air. All conversation stopped. The guitar and the accordion and the bass viol produced no sound. Diana held back the arrow and gave us the same look she must have given Actaeon when she sicced his own hounds on him and they turned him into taco meat. It looked like one of those freeze-frames you see in the movies.

Big Caca stood in the doorway.

He didn't speak to any of us although he knew everyone there by name and would often allow us to buy him drinks until he dropped. He didn't even say *"buenas tardes"* or *"hola"* to the room in general. He marched directly to Jerry.

"Hi, Comandante," Jerry said genially. "What'll you have? I buy!"

We all knew this was Big Caca's favorite transitive verb so we remained bereft of speech when he answered.

"May I see your documents that allow you to remain in Mexico?"

Jerry could not believe the words. None of the rest of us could either. We thought he was having a joke. There are probably forty or fifty Americans living or working in Tecate. They came in search of a simpler, gentler lifestyle, or maybe they just wanted a little magic in their souls. They found it here in Tecate and stayed. They had all their official paperwork done when they first came to Mexico. But after ten or twenty years nobody bothered to carry them or keep them up to date. "Not on me, Comandante, back at the office." As he said this Jerry knew if he still had the forms filed away somewhere in his office they would be dated twelve years ago. Big Caca knew it too.

There can be little doubt that Big Caca was replaying that scene featuring the big ugly Border Patrol officer who called him Hosay and interrupted his tryst with Lizette. "You have no documents? Foreigners are required by law to carry them at all times. I think you'd better come with me."

"But Comandante, you've known me for years. I can't just leave the factory to run by itself for the rest of the day." We all heard the nervous panic in Jerry's voice.

"I am sorry. We cannot make a piñata of the law."

When he escorted Jerry out of the Diana we knew it wasn't a joke. We all ran to the door to see what was going to happen. We watched in horror as Big Caca said, "It is my duty to deport you back to the United States." He put him in his official military vehicle and pulled away from the curb. When he got to the border he followed the same standard procedure U.S. Border Patrol agents follow with undocumented Mexicans. He escorted Jerry to the gate and watched him enter the United States.

And that was just the beginning of Big Caca's revenge.

Not more than a couple of days later Mildred Harris was just leaving Mini-Mercado Perez with two bags of groceries. She was a sweet grandmother type, dressed in what was once known as a housedress, blue gingham covered with daisies. Grandma Millie bought them through Dr. Leonard's catalogue where she also bought her toe separators and her husband's incontinence pants. Mimi at La Princesa Salon on Calle Hidalgo kept Mildred's iron-gray hair lustrous and nicely arranged. The sweet old woman's eyes were blue, bright, and intelligent.

"*Buenos dias*, señora."

Grandma Millie looked up at the sound of the familiar voice and broke into a broad smile when she recognized the *comandante*. They had met eight years ago when she and Fred first came to live here after his retirement and saw each other often around town. "Oh, *buenos dias*, Comandante! How nice to see you!"

"And you," the comandante answered.

"I've been doing some shopping," she said breathlessly. "We'll have the grandchildren over for the weekend." Grandma was nearly dancing with delight at having her grandchildren. The shopping bags were filled with all the things she wouldn't give her own children when they were little; potato chips, chocolate wafers, Fritos, and tortilla chips. "They eat everything in sight, you know. But then, isn't that what grandchildren are for? They are to spoil rotten!" She bobbed her head and laughed. "It will be nice to hear the voices of children at play. What brings you out here, Comandante?"

Big Caca wasn't laughing nor did he join Millie on the subject of the joys of hearing the voices of grandchildren in the house. He despised children. And he wasn't smiling either. "Señora, do you have your documents of legal residency in Mexico?"

Millie still didn't get the big picture. "Why, no. I suppose they might be back at the house. Fred would know where they are. He saves everything. He's a regular pack rat, I swear. Would you believe Fred still has all the AARP magazines since —"

Big Caca didn't show a great deal of interest in AARP or what Fred packed away. "You do not have your documents, señora?"

There was panic in Millie's voice for the first time in the conversation. "No, I do not."

"Then, you'd better come with me."

"Go with you! Where?"

"Back to the United States. It is the law that all foreign residents must have proper papers on them at all times." He opened the passenger side of his vehicle and assisted with her bags of potato chips and chocolate wafers and the rest of the junk food intended for spoiling her grandchildren.

The little grandma was now genuinely frightened. "But you just can't pick me up off the street and throw me out of the country. Fred's at home waiting for me. He'll think I was in an accident. He'll worry about me!" Tears rolled out of her blue eyes.

Big Caca looked at the frightened grandmother, and thought, I'm sure the U.S. Border Patrol listens sympathetically when they pick up some poor Mexican woman on her way home to her children after a day of cleaning houses.

"We cannot make a piñata of the law, señora." He drove her to the border and sent her through the gate. The last thing he saw was an American customs officer going through her shopping bags.

Every morning Big Caca sprang from bed to the sound of drum and bugle calling him to duty. Like a ferret he searched the little town for an illegal American resident then deported him (or her) back to the U.S. He nailed Fred leaving El Gordo's Licores with a six-pack of Corona. Harry Jones, with whom he used to toss back a tequila now and again, was in the optometrist's waiting room without proper documents. This town hasn't seen anything yet, he gloated, I'm just getting started!

By now, of course, the news was running through Tecate like a SARS epidemic. Americans kept a low profile and were getting harder to find walking down the street. Today Big Caca decided he would just slip over to the Parque Industrial and see if he could catch Norman in the office of his cigar box factory. To borrow your American expression, Big Caca was on a roll!

The guard at the gate felt little ice crystals form in his bloodstream when Big Caca pulled up. "*Buenos dias,* Comandante," the guard said with a little tremolo in the voice. "Visiting us today?"

"Yes," the comandante answered and drove through.

He marched into the lobby and barked, "I am here to see Norman Miller."

The pretty dark-eyed receptionist turned the color of an uncooked tortilla. "I'm so sorry, Señor Miller is not in today."

And she wasn't lying. Norman Miller escaped out the back door and was now in the alley hiding behind a Dumpster along with a purebred garbage hound looking for a late breakfast.

Big Caca was well aware most of the Americans were living here on their social security check. They drove late model cars. They lived in nice places, ate good food, and employed a maid. In their own country they would be living below the poverty line. Here in Mexico they used the city parks, enjoyed the security of safe streets and a fire department. And they paid no taxes! Big

Caca felt justified. He was performing his duty for his country and solving the illegal alien problem in Tecate at the same time. He had a thirst for revenge. It became a Holy Crusade.

Big Caca glanced at his watch. Eleven in the morning. He lusted for one more hit before taco time. From his heart of oak the sap began to flow into his veins, delivering new energy and virility to his tissues. His skin tingled. In minutes he was in a state of complete arousal. He was horny for gringos! Big Caca knew his next stop. If he went to Los Encinos right now he could round up a whole bunch of illegal aliens playing soccer or shuffleboard or some such nonsense. A surprise raid. Yes!

Los Encinos is a vast park with a couple of soccer fields, horseshoe and shuffleboard courts, and a baseball diamond surrounded by a forest of immense oak trees. Big Caca parked at a safe distance and adjusted the focus of his high-powered field glasses. He could see at least four gringos. He watched the action.

"Way to go, Manuelito!" Manuelito smacked one out to left field where there was no one in attendance and cruised in to second base.

"*Andale*, Charlie, breeng heem home. *Sí!*" Charlie swung and missed.

There were close to ten men on the baseball diamond, hardly enough to form two teams but the old men were having a great time pitching, hitting, and running bases.

Keeping to the darkest shadows cast by the giant trees, step by careful step, Big Caca drew closer. Inch by inch he slithered like a serpent. When he thought he was within reasonable range he broke into a dead run towards the middle of the field. Now, it must be understood that a dead run for a man of his tonnage could never be said to be swift as arrow from Diana's bow.

"*La migra! La migra!*" someone yelled.

The Americans scrambled into the woods like Mexican farm workers abandoning the lettuce fields in Bakersfield when the Border Patrol shows up.

Within the first week Big Caca's rampage had a profound effect on our peaceful little pueblo and the Cafeteros called an emergency session at La Fonda to deal with the crisis. Present at the long table were the banker, the lawyer, our poet/accountant, El Ranchero, the doctor, two local merchants, and myself. The waiter placed three coffee pots on the table.

"Señores. It is time for action. The situation in our pueblo is *intoleráble!*" the banker announced. "Road construction is at a standstill because El Weelie who maintains our graders and Caterpillars is hiding under his house. Father Ruben is hiding El Smeety in the church basement and he's the technician who services the electronics in our factories!"

Our poet/accountant came out of his chair, nearly spilling his coffee. "We will not leave here until we have a viable solution. Suggestions, señores."

El Ranchero was first to rear up. "Assassination!"

"I can prepare a lethal injection," our good doctor offered.

One of the merchants leaped to his feet. "Look, this problem should go to the highest authority in Tecate, our Presidente Municipal. Certainly he can put a stop to it."

"You forget," the lawyer was quick to say, "that our esteemed Presidente is employed by the municipality. Big Caca represents the federal government. El Presidente is powerless under the law."

"There is only one avenue open to us, gentlemen," our poet/accountant intoned. He waited until he was sure he had everyone's undivided attention. Then he gave us his mind in one word that left this august body of coffee drinkers speechless, which has never been known to happen. *"Brujeria!"*

"*Sí*, witchcraft!" someone shouted. I didn't see who. "*Sí!* Doña Lala could turn him into a toad just like that!" The speaker snapped his fingers to illustrate his point.

"He already *is* a toad!"

"A potion!" someone else suggested. "Babalu could prepare a potion."

"A curse!" El Ranchero cried, tipping his chair over backwards at he stood.

The idea of witchcraft was gaining strength. "That is the answer," our poet/accountant agreed. "I will go myself to Babalu and have her prepare a curse."

"What kind of a curse?"

"Something that would make his ears fall off!"

"I had something else in mind."

"I have it, señores, I have it!" We all looked over to the speaker. El Tacón, proprietor of the biggest shoe store in Tecate, came to the vertical position. "Catch a pompous ass with another pompous ass!" We waited for El Tacón to elucidate. "Bring Big Nalgas Machado over here and our problem is solved within the hour!"

"A cop? Just what do you have in mind?" the banker asked.

"Get Machado over here and I'll explain in detail."

"Where is he?" someone asked.

The lawyer answered. "I saw him earlier directing traffic at the intersection of Avenida Juarez and Cardenas. The traffic light is not working properly. It gives a green light to both streets at the same time. He's probably still there."

"If he hasn't been flattened!" El Ranchero added.

"Get him over here at once!" the banker ordered.

I could see no possible solution to the crisis. If our Presidente was powerless what could one fat local cop do against a federal comandante? I was dying to know the plan so I volunteered to go fetch Machado.

If you've been following the story and not nodding off during the high drama, you know that Big Caca didn't have a romantic gene in his corpulent body. His heart was not a sunny garden where love and kindness bloom in profusion. The garden of his heart was choked with weeds. Life was about women, power, and rank.

He was at this very moment on his way to Lizette who was waiting for him in her Olga "Sensuous Solutions" push-up bra and Gloria Vanderbilt panties. El Comandante had three hundred *caballos* galloping between the shafts of his 1992 Ford LTD. He held the rank of *comandante federal de aduana*, and more power than any living soul in Tecate! And the Viagra was already delivering an ample supply of blood where it was needed. Milton might have said Big Caca was throned on highest bliss. He pressed down on the accelerator.

Big Caca glanced in his rearview mirror and saw a series of red and blue lights flashing merrily. Sometimes the Viagra produced this symptom. But these lights were coming from the rooftop of a black sedan of the type issued by the municipality to its police officers. What on earth! he grumbled. Probably a stupid new policeman who has yet to be trained to recognize the immunity of the all-powerful *comandante*. On second examination he recognized the big brown smiling face of Big Nalgas Machado. It wouldn't be the first time Machado used this means to stop and have a chat or to invite him to his ranch for a *carne asada*. He pulled over.

"Machado! How are you, *cabron*? Haven't seen you for a while, *qué onda*?"

"*Buenas tardes*, Comandante. Can I see your driver's license?"

He's having his little joke, the comandante thought. I'll have mine. "You mean you don't recognize me, *cabron*? You'd better get fitted for glasses!"

"Your license, please, Comandante."

The comandante lost his patience. "Are you crazy, Machado? You've known me for eighteen years."

"Just following procedure, Comandante."

Big Caca didn't want to waste any more time. The extra blood supply was already doing its work in the designated area and Lizette was waiting. He produced the document. "There, *cabron*!"

Machado looked at the license. "Perfectly valid, issued by the state of Baja California Norte."

"Satisfied?"

"Yes, Comandante, your license is in order. But you're driving a car with American plates."

"So what?"

"It is against the law for anyone with a Mexican driver's license to drive a car with American plates."

Big Caca was well aware of the law but he also knew the law did not apply to him. "You've seen me drive this car since I bought it. Where's the problem?"

"I have to confiscate the car."

"Confiscate the car! You're crazy!"

"If you will just step out, Comandante, I will radio for a tow truck."

"A tow truck! Are you insane Machado? Can you see who I am?" Flames leaped from his eyes, steam spewed from his ears like the twin smokestacks at the Tecate Brewery.

They argued heatedly for a brief interval and in a few minutes a tow truck from El Tigre Towing Service pulled into the scene with rotating amber lights and backed up to the comandante's car.

For the first time in his long career of power and abuse, Big Caca groveled. "Come on, Machado, I'll treat you to a shooter of José Cuervo and a slice of lemon. I know you can overlook this minor infraction."

"I'm sorry, Comandante." Big Nalgas wasn't, but it sounded sincere. He may have been thinking of the day he and his wife were returning from Home Depot with a microwave. *Now you know, Machado, that it is unlawful for a microwave to come in to Mexico.* It cost him fifty American. The silver gray LTD with three hundred horses between the shafts was hauled away by the *nalgas* like a dead horse.

"You will be sorry, *cabron!*" Big Caca lost his composure. "You do this and you'll live to regret it!"

"We cannot make a piñata of the law."

The pandemonium in the Diana the next day reached the critical stage. Another decibel added to the chaos and the narrow saloon would have exploded. It was bedlam set to music except that the guitar and the accordion and the bass viol could only be heard in those brief intervals required to put glass to lips and take a sip.

Mario was mixing drinks as fast as his hands could grasp the neck of a bottle. Diana seemed pleased to see us in festive celebration. She smiled down at us from the back bar, quite unconcerned for her nakedness. A bunch of us locals and nearly all the Americans came out of hiding to celebrate the end of the reign of terror. The Cafeteros immediately declared this date a national holiday, and sent the bill to the Presidente for his signature. Like most of their legislation, the bill never passed. We were packed in like jalapeños in a jar. Jerry was there, and Grandma Millie's husband, Fred, and Charlie, who was up at bat when they got busted. In less than an hour Tecate's fattest cop became a national hero. Everybody wanted to embrace him and fill his glass.

It's been well over ten years since these events occurred and Big Nalgas Machado hasn't paid for a drink since.

The Voice of the Cuervo

The legislature was already in session when I quietly slipped in on tiptoes and took a place at the long table at La Fonda. The Cafeteros were taking a vote and the ayes had it unanimously. The new, but impotent, legislation authorized municipal police to bring those guilty of spraying graffito on our buildings to the plaza and spank their bare *nalgas* in public view. This done, they all poured coffee and moved on to the world of fashion but the subject was exhausted when no one could answer who Joe Boxer was and why any woman would wear Joe Boxer underwear. How the topic of intimate apparel came to suggest *pozole* was an undisclosed mystery to me, but we quickly adjusted to the new theme. The conversation took a sudden swing toward the proper way to make Mexico's most popular soup.

"The best formula is two *pasilla* chiles to each California."

All agreed.

"The pork must be lean and cut in small pieces."

All agreed.

"Don't forget the pig's foot."

All agreed.

"Add a tomato and salt and pour in the raw grain. "

"No!"

The sudden dissention came from El Ranchero, and he was vehement. We looked to him for explanation.

"The grain *before* the salt. You cannot add salt until after the grain has burst or it won't burst at all!"

"I always thought that was an old wives' tale," the *licenciado* said. The caffeine addicts ordered another pot and launched into a new area of discussion.

"My wife can recite those old folktales by the dozen," the dentist laughed.

"My wife dropped a tortilla on the floor this morning," the shoe merchant admitted, "and she can't pick it up until after sundown or illness will come into the home."

"I'll bet we have more superstitions in Mexico than any other country in the world. When dull company comes to our house my wife hides a broom behind the door," the banker confessed.

"And what does that do?" the *licenciado* asked.

"The broom behind a door means the company won't stay long."

"Next time I go to your house I'll be sure to check behind the door!"

El Medico put down his coffee cup. "That's nothing. My wife lights a white candle in a saucer with brown sugar and cinnamon to assure harmony in the home."

"If you weren't such a *cabron* she wouldn't think it was necessary," the banker laughed and we all laughed with him.

"But superstition is not the exclusive province of women," El Ranchero said. "I have a *compadre* who goes to Doña Lala the witch to have his soul cleansed of bad luck."

"With an egg?" the shoe merchant asked.

"Of course. The old witch passes the egg over his body and when she cracks it open all the bad karma has passed into the egg."

"It's always an egg!" exclaimed the *licenciado*.

"Where do you suppose all these superstitions come from?"

"From our antecedents."

"But how can a superstition survive so many generations in the face of reason?"

"Have you considered the possibility that there is truth in a superstition?" the poet/accountant answered.

"What you're saying defies all logic and natural laws!" the banker challenged.

The poet/accountant was not offended. He refilled his cup and stirred with a stick of cinnamon. "Then let me tell you the queer story of Filogonio, a distant relative on a lateral branch on my wife's side of the tree."

It was a happy day for Filo (said our laureate accountant), it was one of those mornings one would describe as all is right with the world and God's in his heaven, blessed with birdsong and tassling corn. It was one of those days when you're full of life and just the fact that you're alive is enough to make a man sing. Filo sang a few bars of *Un Viejo Amor* in the company of an imagined guitar as he finished up his chores. He fed his cows, took a minute to admire the new calf, then went to the well. He removed the plywood cover, started the pump, then headed to the house.

When Filo reached the back gate the last verse of the old love song was still on his lips, his soul filled with a feeling of spiritual felicity and *alegría*. Suddenly the love song curdled in his mouth and all the sunshine poured out of his soul. He froze dead in his tracks. His heart stopped beating and he felt his blood congeal in his veins.

Caw, caw-caw!

A big, shiny, black *cuervo* sat on his gate.

By instant reflex Filo drew the Holy Cross in the air in front of him. "Out of here — *vayase* — out! you miserable harbinger of death. Get out!" Filo picked up a rock and threw it straight at the *cuervo*. The big bird, black as sin, fluttered upward, cleaving the morning with a strident squawk. It then settled back down and resumed its position on the gate with total arrogance.

Filo ran at the gate waving both arms. "Get out, you wretched black messenger of grief. No one in this house is going to die — no one!" He lunged at the *cuervo*. The crow merely flapped away and mawked him viciously from a nearby tree.

Caw, caw-caw!

Filo fled to the house. He ran into the kitchen winded and breathless, pulled open every drawer and rifled through the contents. In his panic he couldn't find what he was looking for, or it wasn't there. Quickly he grabbed the sugar bowl off the table and ran back to the gate. Hands trembling from fear, he drew a cross on the ground with all the sugar that remained in the bowl. This done, he went back to the house and dropped into a chair to get air back in his lungs and try to regain himself. He could still hear the cursed *cuervo* perched on his gate screaming his liturgy of death.

Caw, caw-caw!

Filo Martinez was never one you would describe as timid. He farmed four hectares with a mule and his own two hands, and he worked a small blacksmith shop in the barn. He was a young man, not yet thirty, with more muscles than the mule and hard as the anvil. But he was thinking only of his wife, Alejandra, who was carrying his first son inside her. She'd gone south to Ciudad Guzman in Jalisco to visit her aging parents. He would pick her up at the Tijuana airport tomorrow morning. Alejandra was the highpoint of his existence. Every morning without fail Filo gave thanks to God for bringing Alejandra into his life. And now that evil *cuervo* came to threaten the happiness and safety of the woman he loved more than life itself.

He sat a little longer, still panting for breath. But this brought him no relief and he felt a cold wave of fear wash over him. He thought about it. The *cuervo* knew he was the only one home so the omen was intended for him. He would die. He wouldn't get to the airport in the morning to pick up his beloved. He would be dead. Alejandra would be a widow when she got home and his son an orphan before he was born. Tears welled up in his eyes.

In a few minutes reason slowly returned and with it rational thought. I will go and get Marcelo to come and stay with me, he said to himself. His companionship should calm me down and what's going to happen to me while I have someone here by my side? I'll feel safer with him here. He would go at once. He didn't bother with a saddle, just threw a headstall on the old sorrel mare and galloped to his friend and nearest neighbor four kilometers down the road.

Marcelo and his wife Corina were sitting out on the front porch having coffee when he reined up. *"Buenos dias,"* they sang in unison. Then Corina, who possessed those extra-sensory instincts known only to women, immediately said. "What's wrong, Filo?"

"The black omen of death was sitting on my gate this morning!" Filo gasped, for he was still somewhat shaken and out of breath.

"Now Filo," Marcelo began, but that's as far as he got.

"I know, I know, it's a silly superstition. But I'm not afraid to admit I'm afraid."

"But what exactly are you afraid of?"

"I don't know! The sign of the *cuervo* just tells you you're going to die. It doesn't tell you how. A tree could fall on me, I could get hit by a car, I could fall off the tractor, one of those granite boulders on the hill could roll down over me and crush me to death. Who knows?"

"He's had a shock," Corina said to her husband in a soft voice colored with understanding.

"I was wondering if you could come and stay with me. Just keep me company until morning. Then I'll be all right and I'll go to the airport and pick up Alejandra."

Marcelo began to hesitate. He had a lot to do. "Filo, we've all heard the legend of the *cuervo* all our lives. You can't really believe that nonsense. It's never really happened. You have nothing to worry — "

"Go with him, Marcelo." The very firmness in Corina's voice left little margin for argument.

She turned to Filo. "I'll put some things in a bag for him."

Marcelo recognized a non-negotiable mandate when he heard one. "I'll just put some gas in the motorcycle and I'll be over. In the meantime, calm down."

Filo went home, put the mare away, checked on the animals. The well pump was still running so he left it uncovered. He was sitting out on the porch when Marcelo pulled up on his motorcycle.

The two men went into the kitchen. There was a basket of brown eggs and a wooden bowl filled with ripe scarlet plums on the table. Filo brought him a cold beer. "Aren't you having one?" Marcelo asked.

"Not for me. I have to stay alert. Death could be lurking anywhere."

"Ay Filo! You see *cuervos* every day."

"Of course! I see them. In the trees. On the utility lines. As soon as my harrow leaves freshly turned earth the fields are speckled with crows. They've never bothered me. But when the *cuervo* sits on your gate it is a sure sign that death is coming to the house. I'm the only one here. The *cuervo* knows!"

"A silly superstition."

"Not if it's true!"

Marcelo made an attempt to get as far away from the subject of crows and death lurking in every corner as possible. "What beautiful plums!" he said. "I've never had the luck with stone fruit that you have." He picked one up and ate it. "Hombre! These are the best ever. Aren't you going to have one?"

"No! I might choke on the pit. I have to be extremely careful today." Just then Filo thought of something and walked to the back room.

"Where are you going?"

"I'm turning off the pilot on the water heater. Pilots have been known to go out. I could be gassed to death while I slept." Marcelo followed. He watched Filo get down on the floor flat on his chest and turn off the valves. Marcelo could see the poor man was genuinely panic stricken. They returned to the kitchen table and suddenly Filo clutched his chest.

"What is it!"

"A pain! A sharp pain in my chest. Oooh!"

Marcelo jumped out of his chair and went to his friend. Now Marcelo was frightened too. If it was a heart attack there was absolutely nothing he could do. He would only have to watch his friend die in his arms. "Do you feel numb?" It was the only symptom he knew about.

When Marcelo saw Filo couldn't answer he pulled open his shirt. "Ay! " he screamed in pain, pulling his hand back.

"What is it!" Filo cried.

"A pin! — You have an open pin stuck in your shirt, *cabron!*" He put a gentle arm around his friend. "You're going to have to rein in, Filo. Now you're making me jumpy too. Try to put your mind to something else."

"That's so easy for you to say. You're not the one who's been told he's going to die! Come out back and let me show you what I mean."

Marcelo followed him out. They got as far as the gate. And there the crow was, black and glossy, perched on the gatepost. Staring sullenly. Malignant eyes made contact with Filo.

Caw, caw-caw!

"You see that?" Filo screamed. "The *cabron* is still there!" He picked up a rock and threw it with all his strength. It hit the gatepost just under the crow's feet. "Get out, get out, get out! You filthy evil creature," Filo screamed until his face was beet-red with fear and anger.

The evil bird lifted off with its big wings, and jeered at Filo from the lower branch of a lemon tree with complete indifference.

Caw, caw-caw!

"He probably has a nest near here, that's all." Marcelo said, but there was no conviction in his voice. He noticed the talisman drawn hastily with sugar on the dirt near the gate. Already the ants were in ecstasy. "Isn't it supposed to be a pair of scissors?"

"I couldn't find them fast enough."

Marcelo could feel himself start to panic and he didn't like the feeling. "Let's go back inside."

They visited for a while. But they were running out of things to talk about that didn't somehow come back to the subject of omens and crows and death. Marcelo could see it was going to be a long day. "Maybe we should go down to Las Cuatro Milpas and see about some lunch," he suggested. "It'll do you good to get out of the house."

"You're probably right, but you drive."

"Hop on the back of my bike."

"No!" Filo shouted in panic. "One little pothole, one skid around the corner and I'm thrown to my death. No! We'll take my pickup but you drive."

Marcelo got behind the wheel and started the motor. Filo sat next to him with his seat belt cinched up tight. Marcelo was about to pull away when suddenly Filo called out "Wait!"

"What now?"

Filo ran back to Marcelo's motorcycle, grabbed the helmet, pushed it down on his head, and returned to the car. "Now."

Filo buckled up and adjusted the helmet while Marcelo eased out onto the highway. "Be careful, there's a truck coming," Filo advised. "And watch that *cabron* in the jeep coming this way. Looks like he's going to turn left right in front of us. You've got a car in back of you." Filo provided instructions and updated information on vehicular movement in all directions sounding very much like an air traffic controller at LAX. "Ford Bronco approaching on your left. The beer truck is maintaining course and speed." He gave Marcelo clearance for a lane change. In less than twenty minutes they were seated at a table at Las Cuatro Milpas.

"*Buenas tardes*, señores, what's it going to be?" asked the pudgy little waitress who appeared to be constructed of marshmallows stacked one upon the other.

"Steak ranchero," Marcelo said.

"And you señor?"

"I don't know."

"The chicken in *mole* is very good."

"No! It has bones. Do you know how many people have strangled on a chicken bone?"

The marshmallow girl exchanged a look with Marcelo. None to my knowledge, the look said. "Halibut a la Veracruz?"

"Worse!"

"*Machaca*, it has no bones," the spongy girl suggested.

"No bones, but one of the olives could still contain the pit. It's an easy thing to swallow an olive pit." Filo handed back the menu." I'll have scrambled eggs and refried beans. Corn tortillas."

The food arrived and Marcelo watched his friend begin to investigate his lunch. With his fork, Filo raked the scrambled eggs around like a chicken scratching in the dirt. He searched under the mound of refried beans, and investigated the underside of each slice of golden fried potatoes he had not asked for. Marcelo didn't know what Filo was looking for, a piece of broken glass, a stone in the beans, or maybe a chicken bone in the eggs?

"How are the eggs?" Marcelo asked for something to say and saw tears streaming down Filo's face. "What's wrong?"

"I just realized this is probably the last meal I'll ever have with you." He brushed away the rain. "You and Corina have been such good friends and neighbors."

"Now, now, Filo, listen to me. Be logical. What can possibly happen to you while I'm here?"

This seemed to console Filo and he returned to the investigation of his lunch. He didn't realize how hungry he was. He ate it all. Even the unsolicited potatoes. They came home and continued to visit. Marcelo was glad to see Filo beginning to regain possession of himself, but they couldn't sit at the kitchen table all day. "Let's take a walk around outside. I haven't seen your new calf."

The two men walked out the back door and headed for the barn. Marcelo searched for small talk. "I've always loved that big oak tree over by the barn. It must be two hundred years old. If it's ever missing you can look for it in my yard."

"Yes, I was planning on hanging a swing on that lower branch for my son. But it looks like I'll never live to hear my little boy laughing and giggling while I gently push him to and..." A sob escaped and Filo couldn't finish his thought.

Marcelo cut into the emotional outburst immediately. "Say, just look at that field of sweet corn, Filo! It's going to be ready for the kettle soon."

"It's the best crop I ever had but I won't be here when it's time to harvest. Could I ask you to come over and help Alejandra until she can manage by herself?" Filo put a handkerchief to his eyes.

Marcelo let him recover on his own. They were standing under the eave of a large brick barn. A step ladder stood near the wall. "That's one good-looking calf, Filo!"

"Yes, isn't he beautiful!"

"Are you going to breed the Hereford too?"

"Yes, I'm going to borrow Salazar's Holstein bull. It makes a great cross."

Good, Marcelo thought, I've got his mind on something else. Just then they both heard a rumble like thunder from above and jumped back from under the eave as several heavy roof tiles came crashing down and shattered at Filo's feet.

"You see, Marcelo, you see! It's not a superstition!" Filo was hysterical. "I was replacing some tiles up there yesterday and today they roll off and narrowly miss my head. How much proof do you need? I'm telling you, the crow *knows*!" Marcelo was now too shocked to supply a rational answer. "I better get the rest of them down." Filo started up the ladder. When he got on the second step it broke under the weight of his foot. "*Santo Dios*! Death is everywhere!"

Silently they returned to the house and took their place at the kitchen table. Filo brought him another beer. "I didn't bring my cigarettes," Marcelo said.

"Here, I have some." Filo pulled a pack of Lucky Strike out of his shirt pocket and passed it to Marcelo. "I just bought the pack yesterday. A pack usually lasts me a few days." They both lit up. "You realize I'll never finish the pack. I didn't know it at the time but I bought a lifetime supply."

Marcelo did not reply to the morbid comment. "It's dark in here, Filo. Your light bulb is out." Marcelo observed.

"Yes, it went out last night. I was going to change it today but I was afraid to get up on a chair. It's been known for people to fall off a chair and break something, you know."

"Give me the bulb."

When the light went on Marcelo watched Filo jump out of his chair, take off his shoe and start beating the floor with it. "What on earth are you doing?"

"Look!" He picked up his shoe. Marcelo saw only a black smear on the sole. "Look at it — a black widow looking for a place to hide until it can find my flesh. One sting of its venom can kill!"

Marcelo couldn't deny the fact. He got Filo around to talking of his plans for a peach orchard he'd talked about for years. They continued to talk that night until rather late. Filo was exhausted from the effects of the emotional strain but he was afraid to close his eyes. When he could no longer keep his head up he showed Marcelo to the spare room and fell into bed himself.

"Blessed Virgin," he whispered. He sketched the Holy Cross in the dark. "Keep me safely through this night." And Filo fell into an exhausted sleep.

Early the next morning. Marcelo walked into the kitchen much relieved to see his host was still alive. At least he wouldn't be dealing with a corpse this morning. Filo was in his underwear putting up a pot of coffee.

"I'm glad you're up," Filo said. "Come with me."

Marcelo couldn't imagine why Filo was going out back in his underwear but he followed.

"I was afraid to get in the shower this morning. You know, one slip, you fall, you knock yourself out. Many people have drowned like that." He handed Marcelo the end of the hose. "Do you mind?"

Filo stripped off his underwear. Marcelo hosed him down like a car while Filo soaped up. Then came the rinse, and then they went inside and Filo got into fresh clothes.

"Coffee is ready," Filo announced. "Oh, and I thought it would be pushing my luck to put bread in the toaster. I could get electrocuted. I'll go throw hay to the stock while you manage the toast."

Filo got back without incident and the two men broke their fast with coffee and toast. There wasn't much to talk about. "Well, it's time I head for the airport." Filo announced. "I made it through the night. You saved my life."

Marcelo didn't say anything. He walked to the back room. "Where are you going?" Filo asked.

"I'm just going to relight the pilot. That thing could have leaked, you know, you could blow yourself up."

Filo laughed a big lusty laugh. "Well, you were right Marcelo. We've disproved the legend. The whole crow business is an absurd superstition that has been around since our grandparents' time. I can't thank you enough."

"That's what friends are for, Filo, I'm glad I could help."

"When Alejandra gives light we want you and Corina to be godparents and then we will be *compadres*!"

"*Gracias*, Filo, it will be an honor to be your *compadre.* "

Filo waved as Marcelo jumped on his motorcycle and roared away toward home. In a few minutes he would leave for the airport to take Alejandra in his arms and cover her with kisses.

Los Cafeteros waved to Beto, who understood the summons, and delivered the third pot of coffee.

"And so what happened?" all the Cafeteros asked at once.

"He never died and proved to all of us that those old superstitions are nonsense!" the dentist exclaimed.

"No."

"What to do you mean, no?" El Ranchero demanded.

"He died?" the banker asked.

"That morning."

"I knew it! I knew it! I've been listening very carefully," the *licenciado* said in triumph. "Filo left the well uncovered and fell in. Am I right?"

"You are right."

"And it killed him."

"No."

"No?"

"No, remember Filo was a strong man. With little effort he scrambled out of the well."

"Well, then what?"

Our narrator explained. "When he came out he put his hand down on a deadly rattlesnake."

No one spoke. The Cafeteros sat stunned, frozen in place, until the chink of a cup returning to its saucer intruded on the silence.

El Medico was the first to speak. "No wonder these superstitions can survive so many generations!"

"Of course," the *licenciado* said, "the event validates the legend. It has been proved. QED!"

Our poet/accountant licked his cinnamon stick. "A superstition only needs belief to become truth."

The Onion Man

We were strolling among the open stalls on market day. With something of an effort we ignored Josefina's Secret, a display of bras and panties immodestly spread on a long table. We had no interest in the guy selling hubcaps and radiators and bumpers. I was in search of the Perfect Mango. I was in the company of Gabriel Adame, the renowned oral surgeon and painter. When Gabriel isn't operating, he's painting. His canvases capture life in Tecate with a charming direct simplicity and are treasured on both sides of the border. But I also find Gabriel a valuable source of information. He seems to know every*one* and every*thing* about Tecate. There must have been a thousand mangos on the table in front of us but which was the ripe one? I began to feel up the fruit like I've seen the housewives do.

Gabriel reached across and handed me the Perfect Mango. "The perfect mango," the narration began, "glows with the pink blush of a young girl's cheek. And when you cradle it in your hand it should feel like a woman's breast."

I told you the man knows everything!

As we walked away my eyes were drawn to a man seated on the ground skillfully cleaning and peeling white onions. I watched him take each one out of one bushel basket, adroitly remove the concentric outer layers, then place the glossy bulb neatly in another wicker basket. The pungent smell of fresh onions tickled my nose and excited the salivary glands. I noticed his hands as he worked. They were strong hands, agile and sure, the dexterous hands of an artisan, the color of a penny. His handsome face, though unreadable, had the same rich copper color. He wore a bright green cowboy shirt like many of the men here in Tecate. It was immaculate but the creases and wrinkles, the puckered collar, testified that no woman ever passed an iron over it. It was open at the throat and I noticed a heavy gold chain. A little gold heart winked back at me in the morning sun. The required big macho ranchero sombrero was high and wide. His "Viva-la-Revolucion" mustache of tarnished pewter was a badge of dignity and very obviously cropped by its owner. I looked closer at the solemn face and perceived faint traces of the ghost of a man once loved and fulfilled. I put his age at about fifty Aprils. People he knew came by and greeted him according to their intimacy. "*Buenos dias,* Don Zeferino. *Hola* Nino!" He answered these salutations in a rich sonorous voice. A broad smile illuminated his dark face. But it seemed to me I saw pain hiding just behind the black pearl eyes. His smile, though expressing friendliness, veiled an aching heart surrendered to Fate. I let my eyes drop further to see if he was wearing the mandatory vaquero boots of fancy-tooled leather. He wasn't. He had no legs at all.

I diverted my eyes and withdrew toward a pyramid of toilet paper. "Haven't you ever wondered how people get to where they are at the moment that we see them in life?" I asked my companion. "What chain of events must take place to bring us to where we are at this moment in time? I mean, take a man on death row. The fact that he's waiting for his execution matters only to him. The interesting thing is how he got there. What events have to take place in our lives for us to end up convict, or president, or insurance salesman? How did that distinguished looking man end up legless and peeling onions for a living? Why isn't he a beggar? He certainly has the credentials!" I summoned the old woman who sold *churros.* "And what is the meaning of the gold heart he wears around his neck?"

Gabriel stole a *churro* from the bag and guided me across the plaza. We reined up at the Diana, Tecate's landmark bar with a legend of its own, where over a few cups, I gathered the whole story of Don Zeferino Perez Rodriguez.

Zeferino Rodriguez, and Rodrigo Camacho, known to everyone in Tecate as Nino and Rigo, got on the conveyor belt at kindergarten. The ride was over after high school and they got off, at sixteen, ill equipped for the scary rides, the thrills, the obstacle course, or the tunnel of love, in the big amusement park of Real Life. The two friends were inseparable. At eighteen they grew the statutory macho mustache. Together they discovered girls. Then tequila. Then the reality of earning a living.

Rigo began by selling trinkets and souvenirs to gringos in the plaza. He swaggered into Carlos Curios, the only souvenir shop in town and said to Carlos, "Give me a good commission and I'll sell more of this stuff on the street than you ever will here in the store."

Rigo trolled the plaza with ten hats stacked on his head, bracelets on one arm, colorful *zarapes* over the other. He carried a red and yellow hammock and a number of souvenir T-shirts. His pockets bulged with key chains, fake snakes, and other assorted trinkets no one really craves to own.

"A hat meester?"

"No."

"A bracelet señora?"

"No."

"A hammock for to relax een the shade, *sí*?"

"No."

"Would you like I take your peecture?"

"No."

"Oh, c'mon, honey, he's just being nice."

Click, flash! "Are you folks enjoying Tecate?"

"Yeah, yeah, very nice town."

"Honey, I've got to pee."

"Okay, we'll find a real restaurant. Where is a safe place to eat in this town?"

"I weell escort you myself to the door of the best place een Tecate. Good food, good prices. Good bathrooms."

"This is a good place, huh? Okay."

"Enjoy a good deenner but you must not go back home weethout a souvenir to breeng you nice memories of Tecate."

"Awright, gimme a T-shirt."

"Oh, this bracelet is beautiful! I'll take this one — oh, and this one!"

"Honey, you really ought to get the hammock."

No gringo ever got away from Rigo. He saved his money and eventually opened a small store of his own.

Nino apprenticed under Maestro Flores, a mason who taught him to lay brick with precision, erect the perfect stone wall, and set tile like an artist. Nino loved his vocation. It suited his mild personality and didn't require any kind of assertiveness. In a few years he was in constant demand for his beautiful work with tiles and mosaics.

The two friends worked hard and drank hard. They took rooms just across the street from each other on Calle Madero in Colonia Guajardo. On Saturday nights they got rigged out in western shirts with pearl buttons on the cuffs that ran nearly to the elbow. Their boots were elaborately tooled leather with matching belts, and glimmering buckles the size of license plates. Their destination was the big dance at Los Candiles to look for what young men are forever in search of. The girls came mostly in pairs, sometimes with a date. Some were quite attractive creatures, others were cows. The music was ranchero style two-steps and polkas thunked out by an incongruous ensemble of trumpets, hyperactive accordion, an oom-pa-pah tuba, and a snare drum to keep the beat.

Tonight the hall was packed with horny young roosters and boy-crazy girls looking for adventure. The two friends walked once around the perimeter to check out the action, then headed for the bar. Rigo did not possess one corpuscle of shyness and Nino, who was timid by nature, always hung back and allowed Rigo to be his press agent.

"Two beers!" Rigo ordered. Then eyeing a pretty *chamaca* close enough to hear him, added, "And one for the lovely little creature in the blue dress."

"*Gracias*," the girl answered, turning smoky eyes on the dark lean man in the pumpkin colored shirt, mustard pants, and yellow boots.

Rigo stuck out his hand. "I'm Rigo."

"I'm Lupita."

He tossed his head in Nino's direction. "And this is the devil himself, a man too dangerous for you to know."

Lupita extended her hand and Nino took it. "I'm Nino," he answered with a new confidence he didn't feel until Rigo had established his image.

Lupita was fascinated by the young devil in black from neck to boots, and if he was dangerous she wanted to know him. "Do you come here often, Nino?"

Rigo answered for him. "There have been so many *muchachas* complaining to the manager that he leaves their heart in pieces that I have to sneak him in the back door!"

"Don't believe him, Lupita. I'm really quite harmless. They're playing *Adelita*, shall we dance?"

They pranced away to step and swing to the old *corrido* written for Pancho Villa's mistress. His work finished, Rigo swaggered over to a dark girl in a full skirt and a yellow peasant blouse that exposed more than it concealed. They were soon on the dance floor.

The two friends danced and drank until the lights dimmed to announce closing time and the end of the fun. By now they were in an advanced state of ataxia and began the search for their car, a terminally ill 1964 Chevy pickup of no particular color. They stumbled through the dark parking lot until one of them met with success.

"Here it is!"

"You look *pedo*, Nino. We'd better designate a driver."

"You're right, it is always safer to practice prudence."

"It is best not to take chances with our lives. Ready?"

"Ready!"

It was the same ritual they always followed before they got in the car after an evening of heavy consumption of cactus juice. They stood facing each other, arms at sides.

"U*no, dos, tres!*"

At the count of three, Rigo and Nino lifted one foot off the ground. The first one to put a foot on the ground was presumed to be too drunk to drive. It didn't take but a few minutes until both began to sway like saplings in a Santa Ana wind. Nino was teetering dangerously and nearly put a foot down, when Rigo fell flat on his *nalgas*. He handed the keys to Nino.

Rigo fell asleep before they were out of the parking lot. Nino had some difficulty staying on his side of the road until he realized he had neglected to turn on the headlights. When he could see again he missed a collision with a cow by the thickness of the animal's hide. At times, the car would buck violently and he knew he was off the road and riding the shoulder. But he only lost the road once or twice. Nino got them back without further incident. He considered himself the best drunk driver on the road.

This was their standard routine every Saturday night. Sunday morning they would tie up at Las Cuatro Milpas and stagger in for a big bowl of Mexican penicillin. *Menudo* does not cure anything. But there is no better broad-spectrum palliative for hangover, clinical depression, low self-esteem, aches and pains, and various other disorders.

After a few years Nino was starting to lose his enthusiasm for Los Candiles. None of the girls he met there were the kind one would bring home to meet Mamacita. But he wouldn't let his best friend go alone. Rigo would set him up as usual then Nino would dance a few times, ditch the girl, and spend most of the evening at the bar.

"I know your problem, Nino," Rigo said to him one Saturday night when Nino hadn't danced at all. "You're hoping that one day you'll see Estela."

"Maybe someone like her."

"You won't find girls like Estela at Los Candiles."

"I know."

"And what if you did? We saw her every day in school and she never deigned to even look at us."

Nino had many pleasant memories of Estela but he didn't have time to bring Rigo's error to his attention. The lights dimmed and they went out to designate a driver.

The swift wings of Time flapped inexorably and now Rigo and Nino were in their early twenties and so was their critically ill Chevy pickup. The pair still attended the dances at Los Candiles. Nino accepted the fact that what he wanted he would not find at Los Candiles and was beginning to lose interest. Rigo, on the other hand, couldn't stay away. But they went together. Always together. It was at one of these dances that Rigo met the girl he would marry.

"Bartender! Two beers!" It sounded like a gunshot when Rigo slapped the bar with the palm of his hand. "And one for that beautiful camelia." Rigo made an extravagant bow. "Oh, I see I'm mistaken. It is not a camelia, but a beautiful young woman in full flower and dressed in pink!" He dipped his head to one side. "Somebody's garden is missing an exquisite flower."

The exquisite flower gone missing from someone's garden was susceptible to *piropos*. She fluttered like a canary when the family cat strolls into the room. "Ay señor! *Gracias!*"

"I'm Rigo," he declared as though he was saying I am the prodigal prince. Rigo had a way of swaggering with his upper body. They shook hands. "I hope you find it in your heart to overlook my error, understandable though it may be."

The camelia giggled. "I'm Carmen."

"And this is Nino, the very *demonio*. Too dangerous for you to know."

Nino took Carmen's hand, said something pleasant, and wandered off.

"Let's move over to that corner where we can get acquainted," Rigo suggested. He studied the girl in pink. She was on the thin side and yet round where he liked to see round. Her adobe-colored skin was smooth and silky, the hair, black as raven wings, hung straight as string to frame her face. Then he looked into the blackest eyes he'd ever seen, and fell in.

"I haven't seen you before. Where are you from?"

"I recently arrived from Michoacan."

"You came alone?" She couldn't have been more than eighteen, he thought.

"Yes," Carmen answered. "I've heard so much about life on the border I wanted to see it for myself." The truth was she escaped a dysfunctional family in abject poverty. They lived like rats; mother, stepfather, six siblings from various sires, in two rooms. The toilet was five meters from the back door. She fled north in hopes of finding a young man who would be kind to her and provide her with some kind of security. Rigo looked like the prince out of a fairy tale.

Rigo decided to take her home.

"We take no chances with human lives," Rigo explained to Carmen when they got outside in the parking lot.

Carmen watched in fascination while her young *gallo* who represented Hope and his friend selected the designated driver. They stood facing each other as usual. Rigo was so drunk he nearly went over backwards before they got started.

"All right, Carmen, you count to three."

It made Carmen laugh. She thought they were awfully cute. "*Uno, dos, tres!*"

They each raised a foot high off the ground. Rigo threw his arms out to maintain balance. He was determined to stay upright. Carmen was there and it was a matter of pride. After only a few seconds he could feel himself starting to lose his balance. He tilted dangerously to the right. Then to the left. Carmen was laughing uncontrollably. Rigo was about to put his foot down in humiliating defeat when Nino crow-hopped on one foot, lost the vertical, and fell on his face. Rigo took the keys. He dropped Nino off at his place and then continued with Carmen to his rooms just across the street. Prince Charming had her clothes off before he got her home that night. It was a case of love at first feel and not long after their intimacy they were married. Nino was best man.

By the time Rigo and Nino exchanged the warm macho embrace on their twenty-fifth birthdays each was successful in his field. Nino was a maestro in great demand. Rigo owned the biggest souvenir shop in Tecate and Carmen gave him two pretty little daughters.

Without his press agent Nino no longer made the nalga-pilgrimage to Los Candiles. Never too successful with the *muchachas*, he remained single. It appeared to his friends that he would never marry. He was lonely for companionship, painfully aware of an empty place in his heart. He wanted someone to share his life, but it had to be the right someone or no one. *Mejor solo que mal acompañado.* Better no company than bad company.

But one day Doña Fortuna arranged to link together a chain of events that brought Estela into his life. Back into his life would be more accurate as they knew each other in school, although they were never close.

Nino never worked after two in the afternoon on a Saturday. But it was well after six this particular Saturday when he finished a mosaic floor in one of the old remaining mansions in Valle de las Palmas. Link number one. He put everything away and started north to Tecate along Highway 3. That's the way Fate works.

That in itself could hardly be said to be remarkable. But now Fate arranged for the beautiful Estela to attend a social function in Ensenada that same afternoon which took her south on Highway 3 at the same hour. Link number two. But Fate didn't stop there, no! Poor Estela felt the car lurch and shy to the side like her nasty Shetland pony often did to her when she was a kid. She parked, came around the back of the car, and discovered that her right rear tire was flat as a quesadilla. Link number three. She had usually gotten the pony back on the road with a swift kick in the flanks and was now contemplating similar action against the offending tire.

Nino was driving north listening to love songs on Radio Tambora when he recognized the girl he secretly loved standing at the side of the road about to apply the toe of a little black summer pump to the radial quesadilla. Now is that Fate doing her best work, or what?

"That isn't going to work," Nino said when he parked behind her and came over. "And it'll hurt."

"Ay Nino! What a happy coincidence you came by!"

Nino thought so, too. "Do you have a spare?"

At fifteen Estela was considered the cutest girl in school with her seashell pink complexion, laughing eyes of topaz, and wavy hair the color of ripe wheat that rippled off her shoulders like a golden waterfall. But now at twenty-five one would say *gorgeous* — in italics! In the present circumstances, though, she looked vulnerable, standing at the side of the road in a lavender party dress with tears in her eyes.

"Yes, but the spare is flat too, Nino," she sniffled.

"I'll have you back on the road in a matter of minutes." Nino removed both tires, put them in his car, and together they drove to the nearest *llantera*. Nino paid the man, returned to Estela's car, and installed the tire. "There! You're on your way."

"I'll never stop thanking you, Nino." Estela put her arms around him in a sisterly *abrazo* intended to convey heartfelt thanks.

The warmth of that embrace melted Nino's natural shyness like a Snickers bar in the microwave. "Where were you headed?"

"I was on my way to a bridal shower, but the truth is I don't really want to go. Especially with bad tires."

Wrestling with his inborn insecurity Nino tried to imagine how Rigo would respond to this situation. He thought about it for a few seconds then got himself into character. He swaggered from the waist like he'd often seen Rigo do so effectively. "Then forget the bridal shower and let's have dinner." Nino could not believe his own words.

It worked.

They pulled in to El Corre Caminos, a big country roadhouse with a reputation for the best old-fashioned Mexican home-cooking north of Sonora. They were early and were given an intimate table for two under a grape arbor.

"Margarita?" Nino asked.

"You not only know how to change a tire, you're a diviner of minds!"

They both ordered machaca and the big fluffy white flour tortillas native to Sonora. They talked about school, old friends, work.

"I don't see much of you," Nino said. "Where do you hide?"

"I work at the courthouse. Secretary to Judge Mendez," Estela said. "I see Rigo all the time but I don't see much of you."

"Like yours, my work is mostly indoors." Nino called the waitress in the long flowered skirt and indicated the need for another margarita. "I really have lost track of you. Did you marry someone from school? You must have a couple of *chamacos* by now."

"I'm not married." Estela answered, taking a fresh tortilla from the basket and putting it in Nino's hand just as she'd seen her mother do for her father. "And no kids," she added.

"That's a surprise." Nino couldn't stop himself from staring at the golden-haired fairy princess in the lavender party dress that submitted to the demands of her conformation.

"Oh, it's easy to get married. Even easier to get pregnant. But I've seen too many bad marriages. Most of the men around here spend their time prowling for *nalgas* at Los Candiles and that's not the kind of man I want." Nino nearly choked on his margarita. "I'll get married when I find the other half of my heart and not before."

"I saw more of you in school than I do now." Nino said by way of getting off the subject of undesirable men who prowl for *nalgas* at Los Candiles.

"But you paid no attention to me!"

"I was shy."

"I think I fell in love with you the day you stood up to that idiot Barona who had a big slimy cockroach he intended to put down my dress. Remember?"

"I remember!" They shared a good laugh. "God, he was ugly. I wonder what became of Barona. He must be in jail by now." The attentive waitress removed two empty glasses and replaced them with fresh margaritas.

"No," Estela laughed. "He's a *licenciado*. I see him often. He married some girl from Mexicali." She took a sip of her fresh margarita and continued down Memory Lane. "And I also remember back in third grade when you fell off the swing and got a nasty gash on your head. Remember that?"

"Oh, I'll never forget! You put your clean white handkerchief over the wound and took me to the teacher." Nino remembered it all. "I saw you every day in school, but I didn't know anything about love in those days."

"And now?"

The second margarita may have helped to lubricate Nino's vocal chords. "I think I fell in love with you when I found you on the side of the road with two flat tires."

They laughed a lot at that dinner.

Nino couldn't keep his eyes off hers. Sometimes they were the same warm amber of the mosaics he was laying earlier this afternoon, but other times, like when he made her laugh, they sparkled like topaz.

When Nino drove her back to her car, Estela reached across and gave him another one of those *abrazos* to convey her thanks. But it may have conveyed something more than that because it filled Nino with sufficient courage to propose to her.

"I've been waiting for you to ask me since I was fifteen!"

Chalk another one up for Doña Fortuna!

Nino could not believe his good fortune. The happy couple in love made time to see each other every day. They couldn't go ten minutes without kissing. At dinner at La Fonda one night he called the little flower girl to the table. He bought a nosegay of red roses and put them in her hand. Estela pressed them to her bosom, she inhaled the heady fragrance. Then nearly passed out on the floor when she saw the engagement ring tied to the roses with a thin ribbon. They went house-hunting and had a wonderful time shopping at La Nacional for furniture and house-wares which they put on layaway.

After margaritas and dinner and mariachis they took a bench in the plaza and never stopped kissing and whispering plans between warm showers of happy tears until dawn. They would be married in June.

Rigo was happy for his shy friend of a lifetime. "Nino, I don't know how you did it!" he said. "Every man in this pueblo has been after Estela for years." They were walking along Calle Hidalgo on their way to pick up their little Chevy pickup that refused to die. "Estela is acknowledged the most beautiful *muchacha* in Tecate. And you walk away with the prize! Did you tell her you were rich?"

"Pure charm, and a true heart," Nino answered through a grin.

The conversation was temporarily interrupted when a sack of rags came up to them and put out a paper cup. "You look like *caballeros* with a good heart. Help an unfortunate soul," he pleaded in a weak voice that sounded like his last remaining breath prior to expiring at their feet. "A little something for a taco? I haven't eaten all day."

Rigo brushed the mendicant off with a scowl. Nino reached in his pocket, found a five-peso coin and dropped it in the wretched man's cup.

"*Gracias*, señor, *gracias*. May God repay your kindness."

"Why did you give him a coin? You only encourage the scum," Rigo exclaimed. "I have no patience with beggars. Let them work like you and I did. No one every gave us anything!"

"Maybe he was really hungry."

"Thirsty is more like it. There is nothing scummier than a beggar!"

Well after midnight they were rattling and bouncing over the potholes along Highway 1 on their way home from a late party in Tijuana. They'd performed the sobriety test as always. Nino landed on his *nalgas* and Rigo was appointed the designated driver. It was the usual all-macho *carne asada* get-together at some rancho. Everybody got drunk. And laughed. Got into fights. And laughed. Took pot shots at rabbits. And laughed. These rowdy parties no longer appealed to Nino. But nothing changed for Rigo. The consecrated vows of holy matrimony did not deter him from enjoying his macho pursuits.

"That was great fun tonight, no? Those *muchachos* were crazy tonight."

"No more wild nights for me, Rigo. This is my last night out with the *amigos*."

"What! You can't be serious, *cabron*! We've been doing this for years." Nino thought he sounded genuinely hurt.

"I know, Rigo, I know, but I just can't do it anymore. I have Estela now. My life is complete. I don't need anything more." Rigo made no answer and Nino felt bad because he could see he was sulking. "She'll be my wife in less than three months."

"But we've always gotten drunk together."

"We'll always be together, Rigo, when we have our first baby Estela and I want you and Carmen to be our *compadres*!"

The conversation was interrupted when the two young men were dazzled by a pair of powerful headlights. A semi truck and trailer coming straight at them threatened to join them in the front seat. Rigo spun the wheel to the right. The semi roared past but the little Chevy pickup rolled end over end to the bottom of the ravine with a sickening crunch.

It was nothing less than a divine miracle that they came out alive. At the emergency hospital in Tijuana Rigo was treated for a broken arm. Nino lost both legs above the knee.

Rigo was devastated. He put a closed sign on the door of his shop, locked himself in, and got very drunk. He cried every day. "I've ruined my best friend's life. I might as well have shot him!" he screamed at himself. "He can't work anymore, he was supposed to marry Estela next June — how is he going to survive? What will happen to him?" No one saw Rigo for a week. Alone he wept until there were no tears left, only pain that would never go away.

It took courage he never knew he possessed, but when Nino was finally released from the hospital Rigo staggered out of the shop and went to face the friend he loved and had ruined. He found him sitting on the floor, a bottle of José Cuervo within reach. Rigo was too embarrassed and ashamed to take a chair. He joined Nino on the floor. They didn't know what to talk about and Rigo soon took his departure.

Rigo came again the next day. He came every day. He wanted to take away some of Nino's pain. And he didn't know how. He brought Nino's favorite food for him and joined him on the floor though no one ate. Nino didn't want visitors — he wouldn't let anyone touch him. Rigo's help, however, did not humiliate him. He allowed Rigo to carry him into the bathroom, help him to the toilet, and bathe him. Rigo's arms were the familiar arms of friendship; the same strong arms that held him when he was too drunk to stand, the same warm arms that embraced him on his birthday.

Nino was profoundly depressed. But he was glad to have Rigo there and after a time they began to talk again. He didn't blame Rigo. "It was an act of God," he told him one day. "I could have been the designated driver and the situation would have been reversed. You can't blame yourself."

"Have you talked to Estela?"

"Only on the phone." The sound of her voice made Nino cry and he was forcing back the tears now. "I don't want her to see me cut in half. I want her to remember me the way I was. I sent her a letter."

A painful lump of guilt swelled up in Rigo's throat. "What did you say to her?"

"Go find yourself a good man. He can't love you any more than I do but you have to make a life for yourself."

"She'll cry a lot."

"I know."

Rigo looked over at his friend of a lifetime sitting there with half his body missing. Rigo lost all self control. He couldn't hold back the choking painful sobs another second, and the tears came raining down in a scalding torrent; tears of remorse and shame, tears of things remembered, tears of love.

Nino pushed the bottle of tequila to his friend. Rigo pushed it back. When he could catch his breath and felt he could talk without bursting into tears again, he said, "I'll never take another drink of anything as long as I live." He paused to pull in another breath. "I love you, Nino, and I've ruined your life!"

Nino wanted to go over and put his arms around his friend but he couldn't get to him. "Rigo, Rigo," Nino pleaded. "Stop torturing yourself. Life isn't about legs. It's about friends. It's about a heart and a soul." Tears fell from his eyes. "And I still have those."

The next day Rigo arrived as usual except that his arms were full of things Nino couldn't recognize.

"What is all that?"

"Your new profession!"

"What are you talking about?"

"You're going to paint, *cabron*!" Rigo opened a small wooden box filled with tubes of oil paint. "Every color in the rainbow and more!" Another package was opened. "These are the best brushes — boar bristles." He began to untangle a pile of sticks. "And this is your easel, maestro!"

"I knew it would happen. You've lost your mind. I've never held a paintbrush in my life!"

"All the better!"

"Now I know you're crazy!" It was a relief to have something to talk about.

"No, listen, *cabron*! We will exhibit your paintings in Brambila's *galeria* on the plaza. The gringos buy anything on canvas."

"But how—"

"I'll keep you supplied with stretched canvas. You never have to leave your studio."

"My studio!"

"Yes, your house is now your studio. When the *galeria* sells a painting I'll bring you the money less ten percent for the *galeria*."

"I don't know, Rigo."

"What could be easier? I pick up a painting, deliver it to the gallery, and when they sell it I bring you the cash. Simple!"

"But we come back to the fact that I can't paint."

"That's the good part. Paintings have got to be bad to be good. Do anything you want. If the gringos can't understand it they think it's high art!"

Nino looked at his friend since life began. They'd been through everything, cakes and onions, but always together. The man who was sobbing his heart out only yesterday was now jumping up and down with new excitement. It felt good to see life in Rigo's face again. Nino's breast tightened with hope for the friend he loved. How can I rain on his enthusiasm? It would break his heart. It would hurt him deeply if I refuse him and just sit here like a stump.

"All right, *cabron*, we'll give it a try."

Some days later when Rigo arrived, he said, "And what do you have for the *galeria*, maestro?"

Nino, who went along with Rigo only to keep his spirits up, began to regret the whole sham. His first canvas was dismal. Blushing with shame, he held the atrocious painting out for Rigo to see. It looked like an egg sunny side up in red salsa with refried beans on the side.

"*Magnífico*, maestro, *magnífico*! What is it titled?"

"What do you mean, titled?"

"You have to name your pictures and then sign them. People expect their pictures to be titled. And they want them signed so they can sell them after the artist is dead and make a fortune!"

Nino looked at the fried egg in salsa with beans on the side. "Sunset over Mount Cuchuma."

"Bravo, maestro!"

Six years flew by since the accident. Rigo's tourist shop was doing better than ever. His daughters were now eight and nine. Nino's talent with paint and brush showed no improvement but he continued to pour out the paintings. The big canvas that looked like two scoops of vanilla ice cream topped with cherries he titled, "Nude At Her Toilet." The banana split was called "Reclining Nude." The palette scrapings at the end of the day made "Wildflowers in Blue Bowl."

The insane endeavor was a huge success. Every week he sent several canvases to the *galeria* and by the end of the week he had his money. He was making more now than he did as a mason. He hired Hector, a male personal attendant, and Doña Paulina, a sweet old housekeeper who kept his house clean and made him what he liked to eat. He still missed Estela but when the tears came he threw himself into his work and drowned his sorrow in a bottle of José Cuervo.

Nino wanted to surprise Rigo today. He was putting the finishing touches on "The Finding of Moses," which strongly resembled a raw potato in a Nike court shoe. When Doña Paulina brought him a big steaming bowl of home made *albondigas*, he realized it was close to one o'clock and Rigo hadn't come in yet. He usually came by in the mornings and then again late in the afternoon on his way home from the shop.

Nino put down his work, ate lunch, and took a little siesta to relieve his strained eyes. He must have been tired, he thought, for when he woke, the shadows were long and the light was low in the room. He poured himself a tumbler of tequila. He was just going to phone Rigo when he heard footsteps on the front porch. There's the *cabron*, now! The door opened but it wasn't Rigo standing there.

Carmen didn't come the rest of the way into the room. "Rigo is dead," she said in a flat voice. Her eyes were red and swollen. "I took him to the hospital in Tijuana early this morning. I haven't left his side all day. His heart, they said."

The day after the funeral Carmen sold all the inventory in the shop, and handed the landlord the keys. She gathered her two little girls around her and they left for Michoacan.

Stores do not remain empty in Tecate very long. The landlord let himself in along with two workmen. The store, once packed with curios and native crafts, was bare to the walls. The piggy banks, the rude coffee mugs shaped like a woman's breast, the *zarapes* and *huaraches* and blankets and blown glass were gone now. The dust was thick enough to plant corn.

"You can start to get this cleaned up now," he told the workmen.

The landlord then entered the back storeroom, which was even larger than the store itself. "*Dios mio!*" he said to himself. It was packed from wall to wall and almost to the ceiling. There was no place to walk, unless you squeezed yourself through a dark narrow aisle between the huge stacks of oil paintings, titled and signed by the artist.

Nino was inconsolable. He emptied his tumbler of José Cuervo. He poured another. And another. Rigo dead. He couldn't accept it.

Doña Paulina brought him a bowl of his favorite *pozole*. "You must eat something, Don Nino."

"Take it away, I can't look at it."

"You haven't eaten in days! You must eat something, Don Nino. I know you are in pain. But I have lived a long time and I've known pain." She put the soup down in front of him. "And I can tell you, you must allow yourself to heal."

Nino didn't want to hear philosophy. He wanted to throw the bowl of *pozole* across the room... But it was never in his nature to be rude. "Not now, Paulina, not now."

"I'll keep it warm for you, Don." She reached in her apron and withdrew an envelope. "A letter came for you."

"I'll look at it later."

She left the letter for him on the mattress on the floor where he slept.

With wet eyes, he washed his brushes and put away his paints for the last time. It was only fun when we were in it together, he told himself. I don't know what I'll do now, but if I can't be with the friend I love, it doesn't matter anymore.

Nino drained the second tumbler and took the letter from the mattress. Half the envelope was covered with brightly colored stamps. It looked like someone had laid glazed tile with white grout. The purple cancellation seal said Guadalajara. He didn't know anyone in Guadalajara.

Querido corazón,
 Nunca he dejado de quererte. Te encuentro en el ocaso, en la luna, en las estrellas, en la tierra, y en el mar. Te entrego mi corazón. Es tuyo.
 — Estela

Dearheart,
 I have never ceased to love you. I find you in the sunset, in the moon, the stars, the earth, and the sea. Here, take my heart. It is yours.
 — Estela

When Nino went to return the letter to the envelope something fell into his hands. A heavy gold chain with a little gold heart.
He baptized it with his tears.

Tears in My Margarita

*M*ariachis were wringing tears and breaking hearts at the Diana. The patrons (all men) in various stages of emotional crisis, sat at or leaned on the bar depending on the volume of spirits they had so far introduced into the bloodstream.

"What a tragic thing is love!" the man on the stool next to me wailed. "It brings out the best and worst in man!" He drained his glass and I saw the wetness on his smooth face. "I gave my life to save my best friend!"

He was a handsome individual, well-constructed, in his mid-twenties, and I thought too young to carry the bitter woes that weigh the heart. I saw that the deeply troubled youth was directing his conversation to the huge Great Dane seated on the barstool to his right. A *caballero* in all circumstances, I tried not to intrude on his grief either by word or gesture. But then I realized the Great Dane was a life-size fiberglass replica of that noble breed and the poor wretch was unloading his lamentations on me.

The stranger rattled the ice cubes vigorously in his empty glass. Apart from the *caballero quintaesencial*, I'm also known as a fairly perceptive individual and I immediately translated the coded message to mean he urgently required a refill. Mario, a bartender with acute night vision, can be summoned with the simple arching of an eyebrow even in the mine shaft darkness of the Diana.

I arched, Mario poured another margarita on the rocks, and the young man's twisted tale of love and deceit came pouring out.

The scene of the drama took place at MACSA, a maquiladora factory in the Parque Industrial. Since the advent of NAFTA a maquiladora is allowed to import raw materials from the United States, produce their product, and export it back without tariffs. MACSA manufactured all interior furnishings for the Masterfleet Motorhome Corp., in Inglewood, California. MACSA is easy to find. Go south on Highway 3 until you come to a sign for the airport. You can't miss it. It's a blue and white rectangle with the picture of an airplane over an arrow that indicates a distance of two kilometers. Take the road all the way to the end and you will discover two things; there is no airport, and you are at the front gate of MACSA, the repertory theater where the play that is about to unfold on the following pages had a successful run for several months. However, I think we'll raise the curtain on this tragicomedy at La Fonda where we find Paco, an easygoing young man not sure where his heart belongs, Monica, the beautiful heroine of the story, who has no doubt who dwells in her heart, and Vicente, a rather serious young man who must love in secret.

"Another round?" Beto the waiter asked.

"I can see no objection to the idea," Paco said. He looked over at Monica and his friend Vicente for approval.

"I'm not driving," Monica answered.

"We all have to believe in something, Paco, and I believe we should have another drink!" Vicente answered.

They all came to work at MACSA at about the same time three years ago. Paco was in charge of inventory, Vicente was concerned with importation of raw materials, while Monica was responsible for quality control. The three of them knew each other since their school days although the two young men were three years ahead of Monica. They were close friends and went out together regularly. Vicente never seemed to have a date but Monica and Paco insisted he join them. He would usually stay for the margarita ceremonies, then when it came time to order dinner, he diplomatically made some excuse and left them together.

Vicente looked over at Monica. Here was a girl like no other. God gave her all His gifts. Beauty, charm, and grace. To Vicente, Monica was the Mona Lisa, cinnamon complexion, lustrous hair sculpted of pure ebony, a barely perceptible smile in her dark gorgeous eyes. And in the curve of her tempting mouth, the hint of something secret. But Paco saw her first and if nothing else, Vicente told himself, he was an honorable man. Paco sitting there didn't have the brains God gave a duck. He never offered Monica a permanent relationship. He dated Monica and anybody else who came along. It broke Vicente's heart.

Beto put three margaritas down.

Paco raised his glass. "To the most beautiful girl in Tecate. Her smile eclipses the sun, the roses hide their faces in shame!"

"And the most charming!" Vicente added.

"*Gracias, muchachos*, you're my best friends." Monica reached out and took each one's hand in hers.

If Paco wasn't my best friend, Vicente thought, I would marry this girl tomorrow. She is everything a man could ever wish for. But she can never be mine. I can't understand why Paco wastes his time on other adventures. This girl is it!

Paco raised his glass. "It must make the angels in heaven weep that you can't be there."

Paco had the golden words, he just didn't have the soul, Vicente thought. He could never hope to compete with Paco's lyrical tongue. There were so many beautiful things he wanted to say to Monica, I love you, *eres me corazón*, I would give my life for one kiss, but the words died on his lips.

"A little song?"

They looked up to see Antonio standing by their table, his guitar cradled in his arms.

"A wonderful idea," Vicente answered. "What about *Flores Negras*?"

Antonio began to sing...

You are the flowers scented with hope
the flowers I water with my tears
You leave my heart in pieces
but my soul whispers 'I love you still.'

"That was beautiful!" cried Monica, all dewy-eyed. "Vicente, you always know the most romantic songs."

Yes, he thought, I can't tell you the things I feel, but Antonio reads the words and music written on my heart. "Antonio, do you remember a song called, *Adios, Mi Amor, Adios*?"

Antonio played a two bar introduction and began to sing...

I know you must leave, mi amor
I know you must go
Go then, and be alegre
but take my heart with you.
Adios, mi amor, adios.

My heart is breaking, Vicente confessed to himself. If I stay a minute longer there'll be tears in my margarita. "Well, it's time I was on my way." He put fifty pesos in Antonio's hand and got to his feet.

"Oh, you mustn't go, Vicente," Monica pleaded. "This is such fun!"

"I can't resist temptation so don't tempt me. I'll see you *muchachos* at work tomorrow," and he was out the door.

Paco and Monica both ordered *chimichangas* and interim margaritas. "I feel so sorry for Vicente," Monica said. "He would make some woman a wonderful husband. And yet, I've never seen him date any one special girl."

"I've known Vicente since grade school. He's always been like that. If he couldn't have the girl he wanted, he wouldn't go out. I always had a date for the school dances. A lot of *muchachos* went alone. But not Vicente. If the girl he most admired wouldn't accept his invitation, he just wouldn't go."

When dinner was over Paco picked up the check. "Once around the plaza?"

"I'd love it."

The languid air was scented with roses, the smell of wet grass, and felt warm on Monica's bare shoulders as she was wearing only a sleeveless summer shift the color of pistachio ice cream. Hand in hand, they strolled once around the plaza and took a bench. Wordlessly, they listened to the soft hissing of the fountain.

Paco put one arm around her and immediately had to fight back the impulse to kiss her and touch her. There was something magnetic about Monica. He didn't know what it was but she radiated some special aura no other girl he knew ever possessed. What was it? It seemed to radiate straight from her soul. All she had to do was smile at him and he got quivery all over.

"*Dios mio*, you are beautiful!"

"*Ay, mi amor,*" she sighed.

Monica was well aware that she wasn't the only girl he went out with. He said sweet things to her but never "I love you" or "I want to marry you." He made no commitment whatever, but he took nothing from her either. She didn't pressure him. In her secret heart she knew that if she didn't marry Paco, she would marry no man. She would enter the convent of Santa Brigida. Mother Superior Lourdes would understand.

Monica gave him a smile that talked to his heart. Slipping her arm around his back, she snuggled into his shoulder. It felt so good. She never had those little puppy love romances in high school like all the other girls did. Boys were of no interest to her. They always came on like young roosters. Now at twenty-two she'd never met one she could say she loved to the point of intimacy. Not until she began to go out with Paco. And that was two years ago. Now in his arms, she was ready to consign body and soul to the only man she'd ever loved. But Paco had never taken her beyond sweet kisses, never touched her where she wanted to be touched.

He brought his head closer to hers and gently kissed her hair. She scented the night with carnations. "It was a beautiful evening, wasn't it?"

Should I tell him I love him? Monica thought. No! He must know it by now. It's up to him to decide where we're going. "Yes, it was great fun."

Suddenly, by some mysterious magnetic force, his mouth flew to hers. God, she was delicious! Without conscious intention his hand left hers, came up and rested on her warm bare shoulder. In another heartbeat it would have been on her breast. He was saved by the bells from the Church of Nuestra Señora de Guadalupe cleaving the tender moment with their liquid clanging and gonging. Paco reclaimed his senses.

"I'd better get you home, *corazón*, it's late."

It always ended like this, Monica thought. But he was right.

Lilian arranged her flaxen hair with a toss of the head and flew into MACSA'S main office like a Santa Ana wind. She blew right past all her coworkers, causing a vortex that sent papers flying from their desks, and burst into the boss's private office without so much as a rap on the door. She threw her arms around the rotund little man and covered him with kisses.

"You darling angel!" she squealed. "You darling angel!" she repeated.

Frank Freeman, president and chief executive officer of MACSA, was beaming. "You saw it?"

"Yes! I opened the garage this morning and there it was!" Happy tears dripped off her long lashes and fell on the boss's black suit like summer raindrops. "It" was a brand new Celica convertible she found parked in the garage this morning. "And so red!"

Frank didn't mind the raindrops. They wouldn't show. He always wore a black suit over a black shirt with a fine silk black tie. His shoes and socks were the same color and we must assume he also wore black underwear. "Happy birthday, little princess."

"Not so little anymore, Daddy, I'm nineteen years old. Nineteen!"

Frank Freeman couldn't believe it either. His little baby, nineteen! It seemed like only yesterday she was celebrating her second birthday in her high chair with a small cake with two candles. That was the same year her mother ran off with the principle bassoonist of the L.A. Symphony.

He was proud of his little girl. She was always his little princess. He knew he spoiled her rotten but he couldn't help it. When she was little he denied her nothing to make up for the mother she never knew. And Lilian was perceptive enough to know this and never failed to gain what she wanted by a little wheedling and whining. Even at nineteen she'd still never outgrown that whiny voice common to two-year-olds when told they can't shave the cat. Today he still could not refuse his little Lilian anything. The red Celica was worth every penny just to see the joy on her pretty face. On her eighteenth birthday he had brought her in as his personal secretary. He could have found someone with more experience. But there wasn't all that much to do and he would have her near him. He could have put her in the best university anywhere in the world, but Frank Freeman wanted to keep his princess close to him as long as he could.

When he looked at her this morning he was filled with astonishment. His baby chick was now a full grown woman, the image of her mother, and this filled Frank with great anxiety and apprehension. Lilian, he had to admit, was manna for any man's eyes. She was formed in high relief of fine porcelain, fair of face, hair of spun gold. There was a wicked laughter in her hazel eyes, a naughty suggestion of latent mischief in her smile. This assessment worried Frank. She would one day marry and leave him. He never thought about it openly, but subconsciously he feared the day.

Lilian Freeman was having a wonderful time with her Celica. She'd had it long enough to crease a fender but she convinced daddy that in Mexico they placed the light poles too close to the curb. At nineteen Lilian told herself it was time to learn about Life and Romance. At first she felt a strong gravitational pull toward Vicente, but that friendship got off to a bad start. She switched her objective to Paco who was much easier to dazzle, but remnants of her initial attraction to Vicente lay dormant in her heart.

Lilian was at the coffee urn when she saw Paco come walking in with his eighteen-ounce mug looking for a fix.

"Good morning, Lilian," Paco sang. "I see you're also here for a push-start."

Whiiiinne. "I need a booster this morning," she whined. "Here, let me help you." Lilian took his mug and filled it. "Cream, sugar?"

"Just plain black, thanks."

Lilian filled his mug, and handed it to him, making sure their hands touched. "You are always so busy, *whiiiinne*, there's no reason for you to make the trip all the way to the coffee room. Just give me a shout and I'll bring it to you in person."

"You would?"

"Of course! What a beautiful shirt."

"Oooh, aah, er — do you like it?"

"Blue is my favorite color. May I touch it?"

"Oh, sure, yes, of course, I mean, yes!"

Lilian was running her hand over the silky yoke of the rayon fabric when she looked up to see Vicente walk in, cup in hand. *Whiiiinne.* "Good morning, Vicente."

"I'll have to take your word for it," Vicente answered.

"Well," Paco said. "I personally think it's a beautiful May morning. Love is in the air. The butterfly finds its flower and Cupid's arrow finds its target!"

"Not mine," Vicente said.

"You have nothing to worry about, Vicente, Cupid's dart could never pierce your armor." *Whiiiinne.* She blew on her coffee, and turned to Paco. "I don't think even a kiss could sweeten him."

"You're right. I much prefer a *churro* dipped in cinnamon and sugar any day."

"I guess some people are just immune to affection." *Whiiiinne.*

"Yes, I've been vaccinated against measles, rabies, love, and other infectious diseases."

"I told you," Lilian whined. She turned her attention to Paco. "How about a spin in my convertible after work?"

"You know it, baby — " Paco caught Vicente's eye. "I mean, er, yeah sounds good. See you guys later." Paco bolted for his desk.

"Have a nice day," Lilian said and left Vicente in the coffee room.

"I'm afraid I have other plans."

The careful reader will see at once that Lilian and Vicente's relationship was rather prickly. One could never describe it in terms of a Mozart concerto, with charming melodies and sweeping harmonies that lift the heart. It was more of a Bartok free-for-all in B minor for chainsaw and six untuned horns. The seed of their mutual animosity was sown on Lilian's first day at the office. Vicente had been at the customs office all morning and pulled into his desk at about ten. Lilian marched in, and rather officiously, informed him that office hours were from eight to five. The little seed of annoyance grew vigorously and now flourished like wild snakeroot weed in a wheat field.

Paco and Vicente sat at a table in the company cafeteria. Each had a ham and bean *torta* on a crispy French roll in front of them. They shared a plate of salsa and chips. "Haven't seen you since morning coffee. I guess you've been to the customs house," Paco said.

"For a couple hours. It shouldn't be necessary but if I'm not there to watch over them our materials would never get in here on time." Vicente was in charge of importing raw materials and the two friends worked very closely together. He took a bite of his *torta*. "And when I'm gone El Nerdo is always poking and sniffing about to see if I'm doing my job."

"He does the same to me and he has absolutely nothing to do with inventory control. His only responsibility is to ship out the finished product. He's such a pain in the *nalgas*." They both heard the sniff before they heard the voice.

Sniff. "I see you made it back from customs." *Sniff.*

Paco and Vicente looked up to see Norberto, aka El Nerdo, standing by their table. He was a chronic sniffer. Norberto was pale as milk and thin as a stick, his skinny neck unnecessarily long. He wore a sporty polo shirt in a rich melon color with an atrocious tie and purple pants. Norberto, who longed to be accepted as one of the *muchachos*, seemed to be waiting for an invitation to join their repast. No invitation was issued. Norberto sniffed and continued on to another table to have his lunch alone. His canvas shoes squeaked like little mice as he navigated the linoleum floor.

Paco put down his sandwich and took a sip of his Coke, then leaned closer to Vicente and spoke in a low voice to keep the conversation from carrying beyond their table. "I've got a hot date with Lilian tonight."

"Lilian! I thought you and Monica were an official couple."

"I go out with both of them with a clean conscience. I've never promised either one anything. I just can't seem to make up my mind, that's all. I don't know, maybe I'm afraid of commitment. Monica is so sweet and easy to be with. I love her dearly. She would make a wonderful little wife."

"Well then?"

"I don't know, there's something dangerously exciting about Lilian."

"I can't understand why you would even bother! She has all the charm of an eggplant."

"Because she's there! Why do we climb Tecate Peak? Because it tempts us every time we drive past."

What if she wasn't *there*? Vicente thought. "God, you're the only man I know who ever went out with her a second time." Vicente interrupted the mastication process on his *torta*. "What can you possibly see in that girl?" Then, through a mouthful he added, "Besides that. Forget beauty and body for a minute.

Beautiful girls are as common as sparrows. If a girl has charm nothing else she has matters." He put down his *torta*. "And if she doesn't have charm, nothing else she has matters."

"Lilian's all right. A little spoiled maybe, but —"

"A little spoiled! The only reason she's the boss's secretary is because Frank Freeman is her father. She doesn't know *frijoles* about the operation and marches into the offices like she has authority." Vicente took a long sip of his Coke. "And apart from all that, she whines when she talks."

"You're not just a little jealous, are you?"

"Jealous! Ha!" He put so much vehemence in the onomatopoeic interjection that he shattered his tortilla chip. "That girl has more defects than hair! Her only virtue is she hasn't nailed some poor *cabron* into marriage." Vicente took a sip of Coke to clear his throat. "Now, if we were talking about Monica, that would be something else. There's the girl you should charm and court — and marry! She's one in a million, *hombre*. She's beautiful, shapely, *simpática*, and for some reason I can't understand, she has eyes only for you."

"Why are you so ready to get me married off."

"You're twenty-four. It's time you embark on that golden voyage of marriage to the end of time with the one you love." He dipped another tortilla chip in the salsa before he continued. "And you're crazy if you let that girl get away from you!"

"You're twenty-four too. When are you embarking?"

"Oh, I'll wait until I'm sixty to get married."

"Sixty!"

"I don't intend to marry until I'm sixty. Why give yourself a life sentence of misery? I'm not going to get myself tied up to some shrew till death us do part. That's crazy! I'll enjoy my single life, and when I'm sixty and life is just about over anyway, I'll get married and I'll only have a few short years left to suffer."

"But you're willing to see me marry Monica."

"Because Monica is perfect. She's one in a million. Have you ever met another girl like her? No! There are no more like Monica."

"Then why don't *you* marry her?"

"Believe me, if I thought she would accept me I would risk our friendship and marry her in one *pulso del corazón*! But she's not available to any man. Her heart belongs to you, *cabron*." The conversation stopped abruptly.

Whiiinne. The young men looked up as they heard the petulant whine. "Can I join you?" Lilian pleaded. "Of course, if this is something confidential, *whiiiinne*, I will go eat my lunch all by myself."

"Lilian!" cried Paco. "By all means join us." He gave Vicente a sharp kick on the leading edge of the tibia.

"Yes, yes! Lilian." Vicente gushed, rubbing his painful shinbone with his other leg. "Here, let me get my clipboard off the chair. There!"

Lilian sat down and released an audible sigh as though the weight of her responsibilities was heavy on her shoulders. "Only noon and the day is already hectic! *Whiiiinne*, Frank wants me to be sure you all have the office supplies you require." She always called her father Frank. "If you need pencils, pens, paper clips, et cetera, I'll need your memo this afternoon." She began to toy with a cucumber salad.

Lilian turned to Vicente. "And how's our official misogynist today?"

"Perfectly content until a moment ago."

"*Whiiiinne.*"

Later that same afternoon Frank Freeman was elbow-deep in papers on his desk. He heard a sniff and glanced up over his glasses to see Norberto standing before his desk gasping like a mackerel with heartburn.

His long neck seemed to get longer. "We have a crisis in the plant." *Sniff.* He was prone to use sniffs as punctuation marks.

Frank allowed that El Nerdo usually spoke in advance of thought and misinterpreted most of what he saw and heard. "What seems to be the problem?"

"I know inventory control is not my department." *Sniff.* "But my sharp eye is ever keen and sensitive to details."

"Yes, yes, Norberto, define the problem."

"Crisis." *Sniff.*

"Well, then, define the crisis."

"We are completely out of plaid No. 501 curtain fabric and our line will have to shut down before the end of the day." *Sniff.*

Frank immediately dropped everything and followed Norberto toward the plant to investigate a serious problem that should never happen. He stopped at Paco's desk on the way.

"Paco, drop everything and come with me! Crisis in the plant."

Paco dropped, and joined his boss and El Nerdo in those ridiculous purple pants. Silently the three walked into the plant. They ignored the cabinet shop and went directly to the drapery department where they found Monica inspecting a shipment before it left for the United States.

"*Buenas tardes*, Frank." Monica smiled with genuine warmth. She liked her boss. But the instinct of a woman told her this was not a casual visit. She pushed her hair back and moved her black eyes back and forth from her boss to Paco like a spectator watching ping-pong finals.

"How is your supply of plaid No. 501 fabric?" Frank inquired.

Norberto answered before Monica had an opportunity to form words. "I was out here earlier this morning, Monica, and I made the observation that the roll of plaid No. 501 Mr. Freeman is alluding to is down to the core and I don't see one in the storeroom." He paused to sniff. "Obviously it can only mean negligence or oversight which is really the same thing." *Sniff.* "It's not my intention to draw attention to the *errors* of others," he sniffed, italicizing the noun, "but I thought it only prudent to report the unfortunate oversight and save the day."

Monica was also keenly aware of El Nerdo's predilection for error. She directed her answer to her boss. "We have more than enough to finish the run and that takes us into next week."

As head of inventory and responsible for all materials, Paco decided he'd better enter the conversation. He, too, directed his answer to the boss. "I always keep a minimum of a thirty day backup beyond what I know we're going to need," Paco explained. "this way we can never run short of any material."

"I don't mean to criticize your work, Paco." *Sniff.* But we cannot escape the undeniable fact that you don't have another roll in the storeroom!"

Norberto led the way with a self-important gait. He was already savoring his victory. He threw open the storeroom doors with a theatrical swish. "There! Show me one roll of plaid No. 501." *Sniff! Sniff!*

"Follow me," Paco answered.

The boss and Norberto followed. They walked a short distance and stopped. "Now, Norberto, look up." El Nerdo did as instructed. "Now, if you will notice there are four rolls of plaid No. 501 fabric sitting in the rafters above your head." He turned to Frank. "The storeroom was overloaded and we had to put some things up there."

El Nerdo's long neck was beginning to turn red and when the blush reached his face, he looked like a rectal thermometer at 103° F.

"Sorry we troubled you, Paco," Frank said with a sincerity Paco understood, and returned to the front office followed by the thermometer a couple of degrees higher.

Paco returned to Monica and placed a warm kiss on the Mona Lisa's cheek. He wasn't worried about being seen by the other employees. The whole factory knew they went out together.

Paco was still enjoying night rides in Lilian's red convertible and dating Monica for dinners and movies. Late one afternoon he looked up from his work to see Monica cross the office and head in his direction. They had dinner just the other night but he never tired of looking at her. The hair, the eyes, the secret just beneath the smile, started up the jumping beans in his heart. She was dressed comfortably in a slim pair of blue denim pants and a navy blue crew shirt.

"Here's the list you asked for." Monica handed him a sheaf of papers and sat in a side chair.

Paco browsed the pages. "Longer than I thought it would be."

"They're all essential items, staples, clips, tape, adhesive, but so easy to lose. And if we run short of any one item it can stop the line."

"I can promise you it'll never happen." He put the papers down. "That was a great movie last night. I hope I didn't keep you out too late." They'd gone across to San Diego to see "Jet Lag."

"Not a bit." She could still feel the kiss he pressed on her lips at her door. "As long as we get back across the border before it closes at midnight and we don't have to spend the night in the car. Sometimes I feel like Cinderella."

"Dinner at La Fonda as usual Saturday?"

"Of course. Regular time?"

"Yes."

"I'll be ready."

It was an effort not to jump up and kiss her before she turned and left to return to the factory.

Not far away Vicente was barking at someone on the phone. He tried not to let Lilian make eye contact as she cruised by and dropped anchor in a chair next to his desk. He winced. He couldn't understand how such a beautiful girl could make him want to barf. She had everything a girl could possibly want save charm. How could God put together such a fantastic body and forget to include charm? Then give her that whiny voice! What was He thinking? Vicente barked something and put down the phone.

"*Whiiiinne!*" she whimpered. "A perfect day for the beach and we're stuck here."

"Oh, hi Lilian. Yes, that's real life, I guess."

Lilian was dressed in charcoal gray pants and a soft off-white jersey top. She leaned into his arm. "Why don't we stop at La Fonda after work and do a couple of margaritas and a cha-cha-cha?"

Vicente didn't dare move his arm that was now snuggled against an off-white knitted jersey. She had a body that could arouse a corpse, and Vicente was no corpse. But her very existence affected him like a severe case of hives. And he couldn't abide the peevish, wheedling whine that was part of her nature. "Sounds like a lot of fun — who with?"

Whiiiinne! "I hate you, Señor Frostiballs!" she swept away in a huff.

He watched her make her way toward Paco's desk.

At quitting time that same afternoon Vicente went out to the parking lot through the plant. Monica was just punching out. "It's been a stressful day, Monica, how about a drink after work?" He knew Paco would be out with Lilian in her red convertible and he could use the company.

"You read my mind, Vicente."

When Monica walked in to La Fonda she found Vicente seated at a corner table and joined him. "The margaritas are at this very moment in the blender and the well-known restorative powers of tequila, lemon, and salt will soon be doing their work," Vicente advised.

Beto put two frosty margaritas in front of them at that moment.

"*Salud.*"

"*Salud.*"

No one said anything. Each took a couple of sips and began to relax in congenial silence. Monica was, she had to admit, distressed whenever Paco was out with another girl and she knew he was out cruising with Lilian this evening. But was she justified? Paco never made a secret of it. He was never dishonest. It was up to her to decide whether she wanted to continue seeing him. And time was running out.

Vicente broke the silence as though eavesdropping on her thoughts. "Maybe if I kicked him in the *nalgas.*"

The remark made her laugh. They'd had this conversation many times before. Monica reached out and put her hand on Vicente's arm. She thought of him as her best friend and a best friend is a lot easier to deal with than a lover. "He has to make up his own mind."

"But he's being stupid."

Monica laughed again and took another sip. "He's just not sure of himself. I have no doubt that he loves me, and he obviously knows how I feel. But it's going to have to be his decision."

"But you can't wait forever!"

"No, you're right. I've already talked to Mother Superior Lourdes. She gave me a guided tour of the convent of the Brigidas. It's a lovely place! They tend their own crops, work in their orchard, and milk their cows to make *rompópe*. It's a beautiful life. When you look into the sisters' faces you see a glow of peace and love and spiritualism."

"Oh, Monica, Monica, no!"

"I think I will be very happy there. Mother said she would take me whenever I was ready. I'm ready. I don't think Paco is ready for marriage. He may be one of those men who will never be ready. I told Mother Lourdes I would enter at the end of this month. I've already given Frank notice. He doesn't know why, of course."

"Have you told Paco?"

"No, that would be blackmail."

"Monica — you can't do that!" He almost came out of his chair. Should I tell her I will love her till Baja breaks off and goes to Panama — until the moon falls in the ocean and horses apply for Green Cards? No, she'll tell me she can't love me that way. And I couldn't bear the pain. He drained his glass. "Forgive me for sounding like your bossy big brother but—"

Monica took his arm again. "The best big brother I ever had..." She stopped as her big dark eyes welled up with briny tears. "I'm sorry."

Vicente felt the burning in his eyes and quickly drained his glass before Monica could see the tears in his margarita. "That leaves but one alternative. Witchcraft! We'll go together to Doña Lala and get a love potion or —"

They heard a fugitive little melody on a guitar. "A song, señores? Something romantic, something old, something new?" It was Antonio the balladeer standing at their table.

"*Sí*, Antonio! A song to make us weep. Bartender! Another cup of comfort over here!"

Next morning Vicente worked under a heavy cloud of melancholy. It was hard to stand by and watch two people in love make the wrong decision. He told himself it was time to mind his own business and not get involved. But he *was* involved! He loved them both! He did his work but it was hard to be jovial and pleasant to Paco who was just as effervescent as ever. The ring of the phone on his desk shattered all remaining thoughts on the subject.

"Yes!" he growled.

"Got a minute?" It was Frank Freeman.

"Oh, er, yeah, sure, absolutely."

"Good, bring Paco with you."

The boss sounded kind of stressed out. He wandered over to Paco's desk. "Hey, the boss wants to see us."

"What's on his mind?"

"I have no idea. Maybe he wants to can your *nalgas*."

"Sit down," Frank said when the two young men walked in. It sounded serious and when he told Vicente to close the door it sounded even more serious.

"There is a serious problem at Masterfleet. They receive all the components they order from us on time, in perfect condition, with zero defects." Paco and Vicente looked at each other. "So, you're wondering where's the problem? The problem is their own system is so screwed up they can't seem to get their assembly line in sync with the stuff we send. Those bimbos can't get anything right."

Both young men were about to say something at once but Frank shot a hand up and arrested their comments. "I know this is going to be tough on both of you but here's what we're going to do. Paco, I want you go up to Inglewood and set up their system so it's compatible with ours. No one can do it better."

Vicente wondered why he was in the meeting. "Now Vicente, you have to take over Paco's job here while he's gone. You're going to be working long hours. You will be properly recompensed, of course."

"Maybe Norberto might be able to help —"

"Please!" said the boss. "We can't have screw-ups and sniffing."

It brought the two men a chuckle. "When do you want me to go?" Paco asked.

"You leave tonight. There's a flight out of Lindbergh at nine gets you into LAX in less than an hour. You should have it wrapped up in a week. Spend whatever you have to spend. Just don't come back with SARS or West Nile disease."

Paco spent the rest of the day showing Vicente how everything was set up. "If something should come up, just give me a call at Masterfleet."

"Stay out of trouble. I'll see you in a week or two," Vicente said. They embraced the old macho *abrazo* and Paco was off.

The next day Vicente was busy at his desk but his mind wasn't on material importation or inventory control. He carried a heavy weight in his heart, a burden too heavy for his young soul. At the end of the month, just a few days after Paco was due back, Monica would be in veil and wimple at the convent of the Brigidas. She was already training her replacement. Something had to be done. Now!

Whiiiinne! "Aren't you going to lunch?"

O geez! "Oh, hi," Vicente was in no mood for Lilian. "Probably not. I won't have this done until late tonight and it'll be the same thing for the rest of the week." So, buzz off, he wanted to add.

"You poor little thing...*whiiiinne*. I'll bring you something from the cafeteria."

A dark scowl appeared on Vicente's smooth youthful brow, a serrated remark formed on lips curled back in a snarl. Suddenly lights flashed inside his head. The frown vanished, the cutting remark froze before it became airborne. Here was opportunity!

"A ham torta would be nice — but only if you bring something for yourself and join me at the festal board."

This was the first sign of cordiality Lilian ever got from Vicente. Her eyes sparkled, her contours swelled. "Ooh, that would be wonderful! I'll be right back!" She was gone so fast she forgot to whine.

"*Whiiiinne,*" she whimpered upon returning. "They didn't have your favorite ham. I had to get you cheese and bacon. I'm sorry, *whiiiinne.*"

"Lilian, Lilian! The food is of the least importance. Breaking bread is a rite of *friendship.* It's who you're *with* that matters." Lilian was not ready for praise so he waxed on. "Cheese and bacon are but dross for a gluttonous stomach, a woman nourishes the soul and gladdens the heart."

Lilian felt a fluttering in the immediate vicinity of her left ventricle. "Do you think we could ever be friends, Vicente?"

Vicente put down his dross for a gluttonous stomach and took aim for her heart. "In my secret heart I hope we can be more than friends, Lilian."

"Oh, Vicente! *Whiiiinne,* do you mean it?"

"There is only one obstacle standing between us and our happiness."

"What is it, *mi amor,* what is it?"

"Paco."

"Paco?"

"Paco. He's my best friend. I would not want to come between the two of you."

"Oh, but really, there's absolutely nothing between us!"

"What about when he comes back?"

"I'll explain to him that my heart belongs to another."

"I've known Paco all his life. He has a dark side you've never seen. Like the dark side of the moon. What if he challenges me to pistols at dawn? He's an excellent shot, you know."

"Oh, he wouldn't! Paco is such a lamb."

"Within the breast of that lamb beats the feral heart of a jaguar!"

"No!"

"Yes! Not so many years ago he challenged a rival to pistols on the soccer field."

"Oh, no! What happened?"

"Coach Medina canceled the Saturday morning soccer game while they removed the cold corpse from the field."

Lilian covered her face. "Oh, how awful!"

They finished their lunch. "You're a lifesaver, Lilian, you really are. I didn't realize just how hungry I was — I mean how much I needed you!"

"Then I'm glad I came by. You poor thing, *whiiiinne.*"

"I'll need some sort of stress reliever tonight."

"Like what, Vicente?"

"Like you."

"Really? Oooh!"

"How about margaritas and a cha-cha-cha tonight after work?"

"Oh, yeees!" Getting the attention she craved and never received had her orgasmic. "I'll go home and change into something sexy and come back for you around nine." She placed a kiss on his mouth and flew away on fairylike wings of fantasy and joy.

And so began a whirlwind courtship. It was mariachis and margaritas every night, Chateaubriand for two at the elegant Rancho Tecate Resort and Country Club, moonlit walks in the plaza, and romantic carriage rides. On the weekend it was sand, surf, and kisses at Estero Beach. When Vicente offered to be her guide and show her a little bit of Italy, Lilian leaped in ecstasy. This was Life! This was Romance! She packed two large bags and he took her to Little Italy, the Italian district in downtown San Diego.

The young man was giving the ice cubes in his glass another shake. "Let me give you a word of warning," he said to me. "Never stand too near the edge."

"What edge?"

"Any edge!" he cried. "Life is fraught with deep, dark, and treacherous chasms. I saved my friend from falling." He wiped away the tears. "And I went over the edge myself!"

He wasn't making sense. Maybe he needed another margarita. I wasn't leaving here until I saw how this whole thing turned out.

I signaled Mario for a refill. "So how did things end for Monica? Did she take her vows?"

"Oh no! When Paco got back from the Other Side the *cabron* realized how much he loved her and put a ring on her finger."

"And Lilian?"

"Ah! Lilian was no longer *there*, you see. Paco and Monica were married two weeks ago." Mario caught my signal and put another icy glass in the narrator's hands. "It was a beautiful wedding as far as weddings go. I was the best man."

"So, the good ended happily. That's beautiful!"

"No!" The man cried bitterly. "It is not beautiful. Life is so unfair!"

"How can you say that? Everything turned out right."

"You don't understand!"

"Understand what?"

"I'm Vicente! If I couldn't have Monica I had no intentions of getting married until I was sixty. I'm supposed to marry Lilian tomorrow morning at ten." He put his head down on the bar and sobbed like a child with a broken heart. The Great Dane seated to his right showed no reaction to the young man's grief.

We were both silent for a minute. He brought his head up and asked, "What time is it?"

"Twenty minutes to twelve."

He leaped to his feet, grabbed his overnight bag, and took a straight shot toward the door like a running back headed for the end zone with only seconds left to play.

"Where are you going?" I called after him.

"If I hurry I can just make it across the border!"

An Undocumented Wedding

"*Estimados Señores,*" the banker began, passing the coffee pot to the ranchero on his left. "I respectfully submit the motion that we draft a letter to the Presidente Municipal calling upon him to arrange inauguration ceremonies for all the new potholes on Avenida Juarez."

"Second!"

"The motion is carried, señores," said the *licenciado*.

Los Cafeteros were on their second pot of coffee at their customary table at La Fonda. Once again, I must warn you it takes an agile mind to follow the sudden swings of the subject matter that come up for discussion every morning at ten. Minutes ago it was, why does Leche Jersey put a black and white Holstein cow on the dairy's advertising instead of a Jersey? Before this vital issue could be settled satisfactorily they made a quick shift to why Playtex would market a brassiere called "Thank Goodness It Fits?"

Our poet/accountant had a theory but it was lost when the doctor observed, "El Gordo is marrying Adela this Saturday. They weren't speaking to each other yesterday. It should be an interesting wedding ceremony." And somehow the conversation took a sharp turn toward unusual weddings. I told you it required full access to the organ of thought and all your brain cells on full alert to keep pace with Los Cafeteros.

"The most unusual wedding I ever witnessed," the dentist observed, "was last year when Ruffo didn't have the ring at the moment it was called for by Father Ruben. Ruffo thought the best man had it and the best man thought Ruffo had it."

"How did they proceed?"

"Ruffo borrowed a ring from the maid of honor!"

"Sergio!" our poet/accountant called to the waiter. "Bring another pot of coffee and I will tell these gentlemen of the most extraordinary wedding in Mexican history!"

The coffee pot arrived, everyone poured and stirred and the most incredible story I ever heard unfolded. This unusual wedding (said our accountant) has its origins in the highly fashionable district of Mount Helix, in the county of San Diego, California, in the United States of America. Our narrator knew he had our rapt attention. He casually stirred his coffee with a stick of cinnamon, and took a long, slow sip before he continued. It was a rough year for *los* Chargers.

Time's running out for the Chargers. If they're going to do anything they'll have to do it now. Second and ten.

The Mason family sat in the kitchen for their Sunday supper of pork chops, mashed potatoes, gravy, and some green things. Their glasses were filled with a fine, estate-bottled Pepsi-Cola of recent vintage. The Masons weren't much for conversation. You would never use the word loquacious in describing them. They seemed to rely on the sound coming from the TV in the family room to give the meal a sense of amiability and warmth. Today, the family consisted of George Mason, sixty-four, retired plumbing contractor and six-foot replica of Humpty Dumpty after his legendary fall; same frown, the same mouth extending the width of his face, turned down at the corners. His wife, Fern, (age and weight unrevealed) and their youngest son, Lyle, were on one side. Lyle's older brother, Burt, occupied one end, and Merle, the younger sister, sat on her tattoo that said, *Dutch*. (Dutch was history, two boyfriends ago.) They all got after their pork chops with serious intentions. There was no need to talk, they were tuned into the ball game. The vignette would never be considered a Norman Rockwell scene of the American family at Sunday supper on the cover of the *Saturday Evening Post*.

Screen, didn't work. Third and about eight.

Lyle could hardly wait to get away. His sweetheart waited for him across the border in Mexico. There would be lots of laughing and hugging at her house. Her uncle Nito would probably pull out his guitar and her cousin Ramon would be singing old love songs that would bring the big macho to tears. He could almost hear their animated voices all talking at once. And the music!

He watched his silent family for a while and listened to the sounds of clinking cutlery and Pepsi-Cola being poured. Finally somebody spoke.

"Good pork chops, Mother," mumbled George to his wife. It was not exactly a remark that would provoke stimulating conversation. He tossed his chin toward the center of the table. Mother put another buttermilk biscuit on his plate. They don't even have to talk anymore, Lyle thought. You'd think words were grossly overpriced. They even economized when they gave their kids one-syllable names. Lyle couldn't remember his father ever kissing his mother. He gave her kind of a rough hug on her birthday. Maybe he kissed her in their bedroom. Lyle even had doubts about that.

"How's work, son?" his mother asked.

It was the same question and the same answer every time he sat down to dinner with his parents. It hurt him to admit he'd rather be someplace else.

Last chance for the Chargers in this half. Third and goal.

"Fine, Mom, just fine." God! I talk just like them, he thought when he heard himself.

Out of the shotgun...Brees connects with Tomlinson — touchdown! And the Chargers are on the scoreboard as the half comes to a close....

"You still seein' that girl down there in Mexico?" his father said and took a deep draught of Pepsi.

"Her name is Blanca Cecilia, and yes, I'm still seeing her." To Lyle, her name was a song, something you could put to music. "In fact, we're planning on getting married."

"To a Mexican!" George ejaculated through a wad of mashed potatoes. The only Mexicans of his acquaintance were menial unskilled laborers, some legal, some not.

"Well, yes, Dad. She was Mexican when I met her. She was Mexican when I fell in love with her, and she was still Mexican when I saw her this morning. And so, yeah, I guess she'll still be Mexican when we get married."

"They go in for those long fancy names, don't they?"

"When are we going to meet her?" Mother inquired before her husband could put his other foot in his mouth.

"That's what I came to talk about. She doesn't have the proper documents to come into the U.S. So I thought we could all go down together sometime and you could meet her and her family. They're wonderful people."

"To Mexico, you mean?" George snorted.

"Well, not to Sweetwater!" Lyle answered in irritation. George Mason, born and raised on a farm not far from Sweetwater, Texas, came to California during the construction boom twenty years ago, and made his pile.

Mother feared a scene. "Oh, dear me."

"Lemme tell you somethin', son. We ain't goin' to Mexico. All that crime and all those drugs sneakin' in across our border, uh-uh."

"It isn't at all what you imagine, Dad."

"Well," his mother said. "You know all the things you hear about Mexico on the TV."

"You could say that about any country, Mom. Geez, just last year right here at Santana High School — twenty minutes from where we're sitting — some kid gunned down his classmates!"

George Mason didn't want to go there and anchored himself to the subject of Mexicans. "Well, lemme tell you something from my own personal experience, young man. Mexicans can't hold their liquor. I've seen 'em get drunk on payday and end up in the pokey."

"Are you serious about marrying her?" his mother said, hoping they could get off the subject of Mexicans.

"Absolutely! I'll be buying the ring pretty soon. We've set the date for June sixth."

Sister chased a mouthful of potatoes with a slug of Pepsi. "What's your senyoreeta like, Lyle?" She made it sound like she was some kind of trinket. Lyle didn't answer.

"The girl, she talk English? Cuz we don't talk Mexican."

Lyle felt himself bristle and once again wished he wasn't here. Where did this man's soul go? When did the lights go out in his heart? How can I love two people so much, he thought, and yet I can't be in the same room with them! How can that happen? He looked over to his brother and sister who were busy grazing.

"June!" Mother exclaimed trying desperately to hang on to the thread of her original question. "Today is January 6th, why that's only five months away," Mother said.

"And if she ain't got no documents to get into America, where the hell do you think you're gonna get married?"

"Oh, we'll be married in Mexico, of course."

"By a Catholic priest?" Mother lost a little color.

"No, Mom. We're getting married by a justice of the peace from right here in San Diego."

"Well, lemme tell you somethin', son, just so's you know where I'm comin' from." Lyle didn't think anyone used that expression anymore. "We'll miss your weddin' because we ain't going to Mexico."

"You're talking less than an hour's drive, Dad."

"It's still Mexico. I've never set foot outside the forty-eight and I'm not about to do it now."

"Well, I'm sorry then. We can't get married here because she doesn't have the necessary papers. But there's nothing keeping you from coming to our wedding down there except your attitude. It would have been nice to have my parents there. I'll miss you both."

Lyle could feel his eyes stinging. Right after the peach cobbler, George pushed his chair back and migrated back to the family room while Merle, together with Dutch on her butt, helped her mother clear the table. He watched his brother Burt head for the backyard and followed him out.

"That man is stubborn as a rock. I totally give up on him!"

Burt lit up a Salem. "You ain't gonna change him none, you know."

"Well, at least I'll have you and Sis for the wedding. I want you to be best man."

"Glad to do it, Bro, but not in Mexico."

"Jeez! You too?"

"Dad talks like that 'cause he don't know better. Behind his money, this big house with the swimming pool, his fancy car, there's a redneck you never gonna change." He took a deep drag on his cigarette. "But I'm talkin' from *experience*."

"What're you talking about?"

"Me and some guys went down to Tijuana once."

"And so?"

"Well, I got kinda got —" he lowered his voice to a whisper — "shit-faced, and got to pattin' the waitress on the butt. Well, then this big Mexican bartender comes over to me and starts a fight. And I spent the night in the Tijuana jail."

"Well, Christ! What'd you expect? The same thing would've happened to you right here!"

"Maybe so, but you'll never see me in Mexico. No way!"

Lyle couldn't take anymore. He said goodbye to his parents and hit the road. He was at Blanca Cecilia's front door by eight that evening. Her mother, Doña Angelita, answered the door.

"Lalo! I'm so glad you're here!" His future mother-in-law embraced him warmly, followed by the girl of his dreams.

"Lalo, *mi amor!*" Speaking endearments in front of the others no longer embarrassed Blanca Cecilia. Everyone knew the engagement ring would be on her finger soon now.

Even my dumb name turns to poetry in Mexico, Lyle thought. He liked the sound of his name in Spanish although it didn't quite go with his pale face, the blue eyes, and his coarse hair the color of shredded wheat. At first, no one could pronounce his name. Two l's and not enough open vowels to get a run at it. It wasn't long before everyone in Tecate knew him as Lalo. (What would his father have to say about that!)

"Hi, *bonita!*" he answered with a kiss on her cheek. He could hear cousin Ramon in another room singing a now-familiar love song in the company of Uncle Nito's guitar. His nose caught the aroma of *pasilla* and California chiles and the robust smell of whole corn kernels bursting. He knew without going further a big kettle of *pozole* was bubbling on the stove. He heard his stomach growl like a hungry wolf and headed for the kitchen where his sweetheart's father, Don Pedro, was stirring the *pozole* with one hand while holding an amber bottle of Tecate in the other. Uncle Nito's wife, Lupita, was busy chopping cilantro and onions, but that didn't stop her from giving Lalo a fragrant no-hands *abrazo*. Elma, cousin Ramon's wife, was cuddling a sleeping baby in a blue blanket in the corner. Lalo went over to touch cheeks with her and admire the tiny infant oblivious of everything.

"Lalo!" Don Pedro put down the long spoon to embrace his son-in-law apparent without surrendering the grip on his beer. While Lalo inspected the big kettle Don Pedro put an ice cold Tecate in his hand.

Lalo heard screams of joy coming from the living room as Doña Angelita opened the door for their *compadres*, Carlos and Tere. He didn't have to be there to know they were all tangled up in a melee of hugs and kisses. They came into the kitchen and the scene was repeated with their *compadre*. Cousin Ramon and Uncle Nito sauntered in at that moment, Nito strangling his guitar by the neck with one hand, and got caught up in the tangle of embracing arms. Everyone took a turn cooing at the sleeping baby in Elma's arms. Lalo had never seen such spontaneous demonstrations of affection in his house. The knot of small children that washed in with the tide headed straight out to the back patio.

You're it, you're it!

"Today is the sixth of January and look what I brought!" Carlos held up a pastry box.

"Ayyy!" everyone screamed at once. "The corona! The corona!" It was the traditional bread of Twelfth Night in the shape of a wreath.

The children came in, bolted down bowls of *pozole*, and scampered outdoors to resume their noisy games. After significantly lowering the level of the *pozole* kettle, the grownups sat around the dining room table contemplating the corona on a platter. Little sighs and slurps came from the contented baby at Elma's breast. The engaged couple sat close together. Lalo couldn't take his eyes off the girl who in a few months would be his lawful wedded wife, whether his stubborn redneck parents were there or not. He looked into her big honest eyes, the smooth face that reminded him of a delicate seashell. Her hair was a little short now — when he first met her the silky black waves bounced on her shoulders. She promised him it would grow back by their wedding day.

Blanca Cecilia's mother prepared to cut into the corona.

"Cut thin, *comadre*, cut thin!"

"Who's going to get it?"

"I got it last year."

"You're it! No, I'm not, he's it. Run!"

Lalo listened to the squeals of children at play. He looked around the table. It's just a family gathering like any other Sunday, he thought, but look at them. You would think it was a major fiesta. This family just seems to celebrate being alive!

The hostess cut thick slices of the corona for everyone, and passed it around the table. Immediately everyone began poking around with their forks in search of something hidden in their slice of cake.

"Not me."

"Not me."

A tiny clink was heard. "Ayyy!"

"Who clinked?"

"Aaay!" everyone screamed at once. "Ramon got it, Ramon got it!"

Ramon held up the little ceramic baby Jesus figurine embedded in his slice of cake. Everyone, of course, knew what that meant and waited for Ramon to announce it.

Run, ruuun! Yoli is it, Yoli is it!

Cousin Ramon made the expected announcement. "You are all invited to my rancho on Candelaria Day, the second day of February."

A happy cheer went up from the table.

To no one's surprise Lalo and Blanca Cecilia slipped away to have a little time alone.

The following Saturday afternoon Lalo walked through the plaza and dropped into a bench. It was one of those sunny mild days so rare for late January. He and Blanca Cecilia got into the habit of meeting in the plaza every Saturday for quiet time together and to make their weekend plans. He began to inhale the sounds and sights and smells of Tecate. The smell of meat and onions browning over mesquite coals drifting in from El Taco Contento across the street was teasing him. The hawkers pushed their little carts, singing songs of seduction to salacious palates with little resistance to sin.

Talán talán! "Ice cream! Who wants ice cream!...*Vainilla... mango... chocolate!*"

"*Agua! Agua! Tamarinda...jamaica... melon... coco... limon!*"

"*Churros...churros calientes!*"

Lalo succumbed to his weakness. He called the boy over and got a brown bag filled with deep fried *churros*. They reminded him of the glazed doughnuts at Krispy Kreme, soft, warm, and glistening with sugar and cinnamon. He was munching *churros* while he watched the Saturday pageant; families strolling with their kids, some on tricycles, others skipping and jumping, little girls twirling, boys playing chase in and out of the bandstand. Young sweethearts passed his bench joined at the hands. From somewhere beyond the rose garden a guitar played a song he could almost hum.

He'd been working in Mexico almost three years and already Tecate felt more like home than home. The company he worked for in San Diego had sent him down to SIERRA, their kitchen cabinet factory in Baja, as manager of quality control. They had something like sixty employees. That's where he met Blanca Cecilia. The language came easy. A man he recognized from somewhere gave him a wave as warm as a *compadre's* embrace. Lalo returned the wave. It made him feel him like he really belonged in the little pueblo.

He felt a pair of soft hands come from behind and cover his eyes. "*Quién es?*"

"Juanita... Elmira... Carmelita... Estelita..."

The soft hands dropped from his eyes down to his neck and began to strangle him. "Just teasing, Blanca Cecilia, just teasing!"

"Lalo, *mi amor*, you're flirting with deportation!" Blanca Cecilia came around, put a loud kiss on his cheek and sat next to him. She was dressed in tan wool pants and a soft yellow pullover under a matching cardigan. She removed a *churro* from the little brown bag and put it in her mouth. Still warm. "Mmmmm!"

"Have you seen or talked to your parents? When are you going to bring them to Tecate so I can meet them." She dusted sugar from her sweater. "They must be extraordinary people to produce a man as wonderful as you. I can hardly wait to meet them!"

Extraordinary is the right word for them, Lalo thought. "They've been terribly busy," he lied, and hated himself for it. "I'll get them down here soon. I'm anxious for them to know you and your beautiful family." *If they were sitting here watching this scene with me right now they would freak!*

Lalo didn't even want to think about it. He heard the guitar again, closer this time. José Machuca, familiar to all lovers in the plaza, stood in front of them, teasing them with little melodies. José knew them both. "A song? A song of love? A song of parting, a song to fill two hearts?"

Lyle didn't feel like Lyle anymore. He was Lalo now. Things like this just didn't happened to him in San Diego, U.S.A. He felt like he was living in a movie. "How about a song that will fill her heart and make her eyes overflow?"

"Name it, Lalo."

"*Cuatro Vidas.*"

Vida.
Si tuviera cuatro vidas
cuatro vidas serian para ti...

Life
If I had four lives
I would give them all to you...

Blanca Cecilia nuzzled into Lalo's shoulder while José Machuca sang an ode to love. And when the last notes from the guitar faded, her eyes were wet.

Everybody was dancing the Chicken Hawk Polka except all the kids who were climbing trees or out looking at the farm animals. Cousin Ramon's rancho was bursting with *alegría*; happy voices, music, singing, laughter, the delighted shouts of children too young to know they didn't live in a perfect world. It was February second, the day of candlemas, and Ramon was hosting the event as mandated by custom and the baby Jesus figurine he'd found in his cake on Twelfth Night. They were all outdoors under a shaggy *palapa*. The men threw mesquite on the fire and laid strips of beef on the grille along with jalapeño chiles, slices of white onion, and peas still in the pod. The web of delicious smells was intoxicating. A huge clay bowl of guacamole and a platter stacked with warm tortilla chips didn't wait long for dippers. Gay music came from a frilly accordion, a guitar, and a thumping bass viol. Everybody danced with everybody. Blanca Cecilia held the baby while Elma danced. Lalo's movements were a little stiff. He'd never seen dancing in his family. But the music was simple one-two ranchera songs and two-step polkas, so he was in the thick of it along with everybody else.

"Where is your family, Lalo?" Ramon asked. "They should be here sharing the *alegría*."

Lalo felt embarrassed. He tried to imagine his uptight family down here eating tacos and dancing and getting hugged. They'd never survive. "They're too far to make the trip down here," Lalo began the lie, but he was saved by Uncle Nito.

A happy shout came up when Uncle Nito brought out the frosty pitcher of margaritas. The dancing was suspended while every glass was filled and raised and everybody said *salud*.

"A toast for the *novios*!" someone shouted.

"To the *novios*!" everyone echoed.

Lalo and Blanca Cecilia had one arm around each other and acknowledged the toast with a kiss that brought smiles and a chorus of *aaw* and *ay-ay-ay* from the family and a fanfare from the accordion.

"There's something in my glass," Blanca Cecilia said following the first sip.

"Maybe it's just a little chunk of ice," Uncle Nito suggested. "The blender does that sometimes."

Blanca Cecilia dipped a finger in her margarita and screamed when she came up with a ring. Everyone gathered around to admire it. They laughed when she licked it clean and gave it to Lalo to put on her finger. The women and the men all ran to embrace Blanca Cecilia, then turned to Lalo to give him a warm *abrazo*. This open and unrestricted burst of affection was still new to Lalo. It made him feel good all over. He kissed his pretty bride who reached up with one hand and wiped the tears from his eyes, then her own.

The candlemas celebration lasted until two in the morning.

When the daffodils and ranunculus poked their sunny faces through the soil, and timid little leaf buds appeared on the jacarandas, Winter finally had to admit defeat, and left Tecate with a final huff and a promise to come back with a vengeance next year. It was late May and the wedding was only two weeks away.

The air was deliciously balmy. The roses in the plaza were in full bloom and everything smelled of spring and new life. Blanca Cecilia was in a soft pink summer dress with a wide white collar and matching belt. They were sitting on a shady bench for their regular Saturday time together. She could see Lalo was restless. He took her hand and led her across the plaza to where the horse and buggy drivers lined up every weekend. They chose a black surrey with bright yellow wheels pulled by a sleepy bay wearing last year's shaggy winter coat. Lalo helped her step in. The driver put the top down for them, took the reins, and with a click of the tongue, they clopped away.

There are no strangers in Tecate. Everyone waved or said adios as they trotted by. They turned the corner in time to see El Chaparro who came riding in the other direction at a lazy jog headed for the Diana and a stiff tequila shooter which was his custom every day at this hour. El Chaparro looked positively macho in his tall sombrero, dark leathery face, and a huge black ragweed mustache that hid his mouth. He was mounted on a big, black and white Holstein cow which he rigged up like a lot of the cars in Tecate. There was a string of red dingleballs across the horns, a pair of baby shoes hung from the saddle horn, and he had a color print of the Blessed Virgin adhered to the animal's forehead.

"*Buenas tardes, jovenes!*" El Chaparro called out to the couple in a voice raspy as a crow.

"*Buenas tardes*, Chaparro," they both answered. "No more than one now," they teased, "it's a long way home!"

"Fortunately La Muñeca doesn't drink!" he laughed his raspy laugh. The big cow backfired and they continued on to the Diana.

The surrey joggled on toward Calle Revolucion. Blanca Cecilia admired the stone in her ring as it flashed in the sunlight. Her family eventually came to assume there was something wrong in Lalo's family. Perceiving his embarrassment they stopped asking about them months ago. Except Blanca Cecilia.

"Will I ever meet your parents, *mi amor*?"

By now Lalo was not only embarrassed covering for his family, he was hurt. He decided it was time to come clean. "Look, my parents are kind of strange. It's just that they're afraid to come to Mexico. They've heard all the ghost stories. Their minds are sealed with duct tape."

"Do you suppose they won't like me?"

"It isn't about you, *corazón*, you have to believe that. They'll love you." He caressed her cheek tenderly. "After we're married you'll have the proper papers and you'll meet them on the Other Side. They're not bad people, just ignorant. Sometimes I don't like them."

"Shh!" Blanca Cecilia put her hand over his mouth. "You must never say things like that! They are your parents — the only parents you will ever have. Their love gave you life and brought me the most wonderful man in the world."

Lalo had no answer. He squeezed her hand and withdrew into a quiet and pensive fog for the remainder of the ride. He had a lot to think about. The carriage turned right and they were now clip-clopping along El Callejón, the last street in Tecate that runs parallel to the border where Mexico ends and the United States begins. It's a pleasant little avenue under a leafy arbor of ancient elms. A playful little breeze came up and a million leaves applauded the couple in love.

On Lalo's left stretched a vast sea of empty land behind four strands of barbed wire that separate two sovereign nations, each with its own language, each steeped in its own prejudicial views of the other. Someone was using the fence for a clothesline today. Red and yellow blankets were draped over the wire. On his right stood Tecate's oldest houses looking out at the follies of the young with the tolerance and wisdom of grandparents who have seen it all before and aren't impressed. He contemplated the endless rows of steel fenceposts as they drifted past. He looked to the north where men were afraid to reveal their feelings, then to the south, where the toughest macho would sing along with a love song with tears in his eyes if the music touched his heart. People out watering their gardens, or sweeping their patios, or washing the car, stopped what they were doing to wave adios. Little girls jumping rope interrupted their game to stare in wonderment at the couple in the carriage.

Finally, Lalo spoke. "Our wedding is going off as scheduled," he said. "If they're not here, it's their loss."

The carriage lurched suddenly as the shaggy bay spooked at the sight of a bunch of boys playing a rowdy game of soccer in the middle of the street. Quickly, the driver checked the horse and held him tightly while a kid booted the ball with all his strength. Lalo watched the ball go wide, fly over the fence, and enter the United States illegally. The boys suspended their game while the driver coaxed the nervous horse safely around the corner and they clopped along the quiet street adjacent to the cemetery.

When they got back to the plaza Lalo helped her step down and paid the driver.

"Ready for an ice cream?"

"*Sí!*"

They took a small table at the Flor de Michoacan. Lalo came back with two cups filled with fresh mango ice cream.

Blanca Cecilia reached out for his hand. "What is it, *mi amor*? You're so quiet. You haven't said a word."

"I think I just solved our problem."

"You mean, your family will actually attend our wedding?"

"Yes."

"Really, your whole family?"

"All of them."

A chorus of angel voices sang *Ave Maria*.

The bride in shimmering white satin and frothy veil walked between velvet ropes and down the runner of red carpet on her father's arm. Blanca Cecilia looked frail and pure, Don Pedro beamed with pride.

Lalo, a tangle of nerves in black cutaway tuxedo, waited for his bride near the justice, his brother Burt at his side. Six bridesmaids in peach-colored gowns fanned out as the bride and her father approached the justice. Lalo looked out at the crowd of faces. Every seat was taken. There was her entire family. He could make out Doña Angelita, Uncle Nito, and Ramon. He recognized everyone from the Twelfth Night fiesta. His eyes turned toward the groom's side.

And there they were; Dad, Mother, his sister with her latest boyfriend, and next to her, Burt's girlfriend.

"Dearly beloved, we are gathered here before God..."

Lalo admitted later that his mind deserted him and left him abandoned at the altar. He never regained consciousness until Burt nudged him sharply in the ribs and he heard the words, "I pronounce you man and wife. You may kiss the bride."

Lalo leaned over the four strands of barbed wire fence that ran between him standing in the United States of America, and his beautiful bride standing in Mexico. Reverently, he raised the diaphanous veil, and consecrated the marriage with a kiss. Almost at once it began to rain rice.

And the festive music of mariachis fluttered down on two countries like confetti at a fiesta.

A Note from the Author

One dismally cold and frosty morning, cold enough to numb unwanted thoughts and freeze the ears off a polar bear, I was out, machete in hand, cutting kindling to appease the insatiable appetite of five fireplaces and a monster wood-burning kitchen range. While employed in this perpetual endeavor I came upon a red balloon in the shape of a heart that, for lack of helium, crash-landed in the chaparral here on the rancho. It was damp with morning dew, or tears, and it looked exhausted. I untangled it from the brush and as I pulled it out I saw there was a note attached. It began, "Dear God." I won't reveal the nature of the petition or the name of the signer. I can only hope the Mylar herald angel had satisfactorily consummated his entrusted commission with the Lord before falling back to earth.

Later in the afternoon, I poured two amber fingers of Jameson, settled down before an aromatic fire of eucalyptus logs, and recorded the event on the back of several envelopes until I found my yellow pad. This simple exercise spawned the book you now hold in your hands. The note, and what remains of the ribbon, sits in a small gold frame on my mantelpiece. The events on the foregoing pages are all true. I don't really write my stories, I *see* them. All the characters are real. Judiciously, I have baptized them with new names of my own invention, ostensibly so that I may continue to enjoy an uncomplicated life in Tecate. Some stories can be dangerous to tell.

Remember Esperanza? She presented Salvador with an adorable baby girl, her little head crowned with a mass of curls the color of the old ten-peso gold pieces of long ago. Father Ruben baptized her Milagro. Lucrecia has a good job in the cafeteria at the new Toyota factory. She became a grandmother at thirty-four when Carmen had a boy at sixteen. It's been a struggle for Carmen, but Magali and Pilar are properly married to good men. Betito no longer plays in the dirt with a toy car. He's in his first year of law school at the University of Tijuana. No one's seen Fermin and I heard Lydia moved to Mexicali and married a *licenciado*. Big Caca is history, I'm happy to say, and Big Nalgas Machado is still wallowing in praise. I still see the Onion Man almost every day sitting on the floor cleaning onions at the *fruteria*. I look into his eyes and see echoes of the past and a little starburst from the gold heart resting at his throat. I attended a *carne asada* fiesta at Uncle Nino's ranch and ran into Lalo and Blanca Cecilia and their two handsome children. They are expecting a third, and judging from her appearance, it may have arrived just after I left.

Nothing exciting ever happens here. The traditional nativity scene was set out in the plaza as usual. But this year it was done with live animals for the first time. Paper maché shepherds tended their living flocks. Fiberglass Wisemen knelt before the newborn King. The ceramic figures of Joseph and Mary were beautifully lifelike. And the porcelain baby Jesus wrapped in swaddling clothes lay asleep in the manger. The whole scene looked like Domenico Ghirlandaio's "Adoration of the Magi" at the Uffizi in Florence. The Scriptures cite numerous examples of wayward sheep, sheep that stray from the fold and get lost and get into trouble. Well, one day these sheep did indeed wander from their guardian shepherds and began to ravage the hay in the manger. It became necessary to fence off the Holy Family.

The Cafeteros, those incorrigible rhetoricians, still hold court at La Fonda every morning to write their ludicrous legislation and tell their outrageous stories over several pots of coffee. I joined them this past Sixth of January, Day of the Reyes. They were passing out generous slices of the corona from the bakery across the plaza. I was obliged to accept a slice. That may have been a mistake. I got the piece with the miniature figure of the

Lord Jesus in it. I will be ladling out big bowls of *pozole* and serving up tequila, lemon, and salt to slake the thirst of eleven chronically parched Cafeteros here on my rancho come the Day of Candelaria, February 2nd.

I got back to the rancho rather late last night and there was a big brown owl sitting on the lower branch of the old ash tree that stands guard at the entrance to the villa. *Tu-whoo, tu-whoo.* I won't bother to tell you the rest. You wouldn't believe it anyway.

— *D.R.*

Tecate, B.C.N., Mexico
2004

*M*exican author Daniel Reveles invites us to join him at his corner table at La Fonda for another helping of tales in *Tequila, Lemon, and Salt.* His previous books, *Enchiladas, Rice, and Beans* and *Salsa and Chips,* appear on required reading lists across the country. He enjoys a diversified audience of both non-Latino and Latino readers, probably

PHOTO: MARK REVELES

because he takes the former to where they've never been, and the latter to where they *have* been.

Reveles began his career at Paramount Pictures in Hollywood as a "script girl," and remained in some aspect of the entertainment industry for many years, as a recording artist, songwriter, television producer, and disc jockey. He is credited with introducing the infectious Cuban rhythms of cha-cha-cha and merengue to the Los Angeles market, when no one else would, on his Spanish-language radio show "Fiesta Latina."

Twenty-five years ago, Reveles got lost on his way to Ensenada, stumbled into Tecate, fell in love with the pueblo, and has remained ever since. He lives among jackrabbits and coyotes on a remote hacienda on the outskirts of town. When he isn't writing he plays chamber music, throws paint at a canvas, and can be seen roaming the plaza for new material or doing damage to a plate of cactus and eggs at La Tradicion. He is presently in a stormy relationship with a computer, and can be reached via e–mail at dreveles@pacbell.net.

Sunbelt Publications'
Baja California Booklist

"Adventures in the Natural History and
Cultural Heritage of The Californias"
A Series Edited by Lowell Lindsay

Antigua California (University of New Mexico Press)   Crosby
The definitive history of the peninsula's mission and colonial frontier period.

Backroad Baja: The Central Region   Higginbotham
Twenty offroad trips to Baja California's beaches, missions and ranchos.

Baja Legends: Historic Characters, Events, Locations Niemann
The author's extensive knowledge of Baja's colorful past and booming present.

Baja Outpost: The Guest Book from Patchen's Cabin   Patchen
Stories, reminiscences, and comments from the remote cabin's many guests.

Cave Paintings of Baja California, Rev. Ed.   Crosby
A full-color account of the author's exploration of world-class rock art sites.

Gateway to Alta California: The 1769 Expedition   Crosby
The groundbreaking trek through northern Baja California.
Color maps.

Houses of Los Cabos (Amaroma)   Aldrete
A stunning full-color pictorial highlighting architecture in and near the Cape.

Journey with a Baja Burro   Mackintosh
Over 1,000 miles on foot, with his trusty companion, from Tecate to Loreto.

Loreto, Baja California (Tio Press)   O'Neil
A comprehensive history of the small town that was California's
first mission and Capital.

Lost Cabos: The Way it Was (Lost Cabos Press) Jackson
A memoir of doing business in the 60s and 70s in the former
fishing village.

Mexican Slang Plus Graffiti   Robinson
The hip talk and off-color eloquence of the Spanish commonly
used in Mexico.

Mexicoland: Stories from Todos Santos (Barking Dog) Mercer
These stories, ranging from satirical to dramatic, capture daily
life in Baja.

Spanish Lingo for the Savvy Gringo   Reid
The colloquial Spanish of Mexico, plus a guide to language and
customs.

Tequila, Lemon, and Salt   Reveles
The border town of Tecate comes to colorful life in this collection
of stories.

The Other Side: Journeys In Baja California Botello
Over twenty years of traveling—a love story, adventure, and inner
journey.

The Baja California Travel Series (Dawson) Various authors
More than a dozen titles in this hard-to-find series of histories.

We carry hundreds of books on Baja California,
Mexico, and the Southwest U.S.!

www.sunbeltbooks.com